# Sixth Grade Secrets

*Sideways Arithmetic from Wayside School*
**Louis Sachar**

*More Sideways Arithmetic from Wayside School*
**Louis Sachar**

*Report to the Principal's Office*
**Jerry Spinelli**

*Who Ran My Underwear Up the Flagpole?*
**Jerry Spinelli**

*Picklemania*
**Jerry Spinelli**

*Do the Funky Pickle*
**Jerry Spinelli**

*The Library Card*
**Jerry Spinelli**

*Fourth Grade Rats*
**Jerry Spinelli**

# Sixth Grade Secrets

## LOUIS SACHAR

AN
**APPLE**
PAPERBACK

SCHOLASTIC INC.
New York   Toronto   London   Auckland   Sydney
Mexico City   New Delhi   Hong Kong   Buenos Aires

ISBN 0-590-46075-7

12 11 10 9 8 7 6 5 4 3 2          4 5 6 7 8 9/0

Printed in the U.S.A.          40

*Dedicated, with love,
to Sherre Madelyn Sachar,
on her one-month birthday.*

# Table of Characters

*This is a list* of some of the people in Laura's class. Laura has been going to the same school for over six years, so she knows everybody there fairly well. But unless you happen to go to Laura's school, you may have trouble remembering who is who. This list is here to help you if you need it. These aren't all the people in Laura's class, just the ones who are mentioned in the book at least twice.

*Laura* -— Our hero. If you forget who she is, then you'll need more than this list to help you.

*Tiffany* — Ticklish. Has trouble eating spaghetti.

*Allison* — Always wears clean underwear.

*Gabriel* — Has copied more dictionary pages than anyone else in Mr. Doyle's class.

*Mr. Doyle* — The best teacher in the school.

The worst teacher in the school. Take your pick.

*Kristin* — Small face, big glasses.

*Sheila* — Frizzy hair. Hates Laura. Sits behind Gabriel.

*Debbie* — Hangs upside-down before tests.

*Howard* — Wants everybody to like him. Nobody does.

*Karen* — Talks all the time. Yolanda's best friend. Nothing bothers her, not even Gabriel.

*Yolanda* — Very shy. Very pretty. Karen's best friend.

*Jonathan* — Smartest, fastest, strongest, and most handsome boy in Mr. Doyle's class, and he knows it.

*Nathan* — Talks funny. Likes to watch turkeys play football.

*Aaron* — Good singer. His grandmother picks out his clothes for him.

*Linzy* — Teacher's pet. Has never had to copy a dictionary page.

There are fifteen other kids in Mr. Doyle's class who didn't make this list. I hope they don't feel too bad. I'm sure they are interesting people, too, and maybe someday some other author will write a story about them.

# PART ONE

# The Treasures of Pig City

# 1
# Laura

*It all started* with a hat.

Laura was at a garage sale with her friends Tiffany and Allison.

"Euu, don't put that on your head," said Allison. "You don't know where it's been. It might have lice."

Laura hesitated a moment, then put it on her head. She realized Allison might be right, but she also thought it was a tacky thing to say in front of the man who used to wear it. Anyway, the man was bald, so how could he have lice?

"How much?" she asked.

The bald man smiled. He was missing a front tooth. "Well, it was a dollar," he said, "but since you're so pretty, you can have it for fifty cents."

It was a red cap with a blue brim. In silver letters

above the brim were the words PIG CITY. It fit snug, but not too tight over her very long brown hair.

"What do you think?" she asked her friends.

Tiffany looked up from a box of records and laughed. "It's cute," she said.

"Everything looks cute on you, Laura," Allison agreed.

Laura bought the cap, but she insisted on paying the original price, one dollar. She didn't think she should get it any cheaper just because she was pretty.

"What does Pig City mean?" Tiffany asked the man.

He didn't answer. He just winked at her.

Laura knew her parents wouldn't like the cap. They never liked any clothes she bought at garage sales. They couldn't understand why she'd want to wear somebody's old clothes when they'd buy her anything she wanted new.

But where would she be able to find a new cap that said PIG CITY on it? Well, actually, she remembered there was a store at the mall where they sold caps with anything anyone wanted printed on them. Still, it wasn't the same. The thing that made this cap so special was that she didn't buy it at the mall. It was like Allison had said, "You don't know where it's been." That was why she liked it. What was Pig City? It was mysterious.

"How do you know it doesn't have lice?" Allison asked as the three girls walked away.

"He was bald," said Laura.

"So?" asked Allison. "He wasn't *always* bald."

"How do you know?" asked Tiffany. "Maybe he was born bald."

"Everybody's born bald," said Laura.

Tiffany laughed.

"Well, I wouldn't put someone else's hat on my head," said Allison. "What if the man used to be a pig farmer?"

Allison had short brown hair, neatly combed and parted just a little off center. Her face was clean, fresh, and healthy-looking. Her teeth were white, and her fingernails were neatly trimmed. You could tell just by looking at her that she always wore clean underwear.

"Maybe Pig City is the name of a health club," said Tiffany, "where fat people go to lose weight."

Allison laughed. "Or where slobs go to learn good manners," she added.

Laura laughed.

"What if it really is a city?" asked Tiffany. "And the only people who live there are fat slobs with bad manners!"

They all laughed.

"Maybe it's a beautiful city," said Laura, "with flowers everywhere, and trees and beaches. They just call it Pig City to keep the tourists away."

"Wouldn't that be great?" said Allison. "And not too many people would want to live in a city named Pig City, either, so it's not crowded or polluted."

"It's the most wonderful place in the world," said Tiffany, "just like the Garden of Eden. And nobody wears clothes, just fig leaves."

Tiffany probably changed her underwear every day, too, only you couldn't tell just by looking at her. Something about her was always messy. Her clothes never fit right. The more she tried to comb her hair, the worse it got.

"I'm going to be a pig farmer when I grow up," Laura declared.

Tiffany laughed.

"I thought you wanted to be President," said Allison.

"I can do both," said Laura. "You're only allowed to be President for eight years."

Laura's goal was to be the first woman President of the United States. That was why it bothered her when people told her she was pretty. Nobody ever told George Washington he was pretty!

Laura had little doubt that she would someday be President. It was just a question of whether or not she'd be the first woman. She was afraid another woman might beat her to it.

Just as George Washington is known as the Father of our Country, someday she wanted to be known as the Mother of our Country.

"If you're a pig farmer, you'll have to kill pigs," Tiffany pointed out.

"Oh, I could never do that," said Laura.

"That's how they make their money," said Tiffany. "They raise pigs until they're big and fat, then they butcher them! Just so people can eat bacon. It's disgusting."

"What about the farmers who just have dairy cows?" asked Allison. "They don't kill their cows. They just milk them and make money by selling the milk."

"But Laura wants to be a pig farmer, not a cow farmer," said Tiffany.

"Oh," said Allison. "So?" she asked. "Why can't

she milk pigs? Pigs are mammals! They have milk, too."

They had been studying mammals in Mr. Doyle's class.

"Pig milk?" questioned Tiffany.

"Yes!" exclaimed Laura. She liked that idea. "You've heard of goat milk. Why not pig milk? It will be a new product! And pig cheese! I'll be the only one selling it, so I'll make lots of money."

"How about pig yogurt?" suggested Allison. "Yogurt already tastes like it comes from pigs, anyway."

"And pig butter," said Laura.

"And pig cottage cheese," said Allison.

"And pig ice cream," Tiffany joined in.

When Laura was four years old her father told her about George Washington. It was the day before her first day of kindergarten. She was supposed to get her hair cut. She threw a temper tantrum.

"No!" she screamed and cried. "I don't want to get my hair cut! No! No! No! No! No!" She stomped angrily around the house, kicking things. When she kicked a table in the living room, the lamp on top of it fell and broke.

She instantly stopped crying.

Her father rushed in when he heard the crash. He looked at Laura, then at the broken lamp. "How did this happen?" he demanded.

"I don't know, Daddy," Laura said innocently. "I was just standing here, when suddenly the lamp broke."

He didn't get angry or accuse her of lying. Instead, he told her the story of George Washington and the cherry tree, and how George later grew up to be the first President of the United States, the Father of our Country!

When he finished, Laura stared bravely into her father's eyes and said, "I cannot tell a lie. I broke the lamp."

Just as George Washington didn't get in trouble for chopping down the cherry tree, Laura Sibbie didn't get in trouble for breaking the lamp. She didn't have to get her hair cut, either. Her parents promised she'd never have to get her hair cut, as long as she never told another lie.

She was now in the sixth grade. There was only a month and a half left of school. Her hair was long and thick and reached down below her waist. She hadn't lied yet.

"Pig ice cream?" questioned Allison. "Yuck-ola!"

# 2
# Pig City

*Laura wore the cap* every day for a week. Her parents got used to it. Everybody in school made some dumb comment about it, but soon they got used to it, too. By the end of the week, it had become a part of her. She would have looked strange without it.

"We'll be in the Dog House!" Laura shouted, then slammed the door behind her.

Tiffany and Allison were waiting in the backyard, sucking on grape popsicles. They liked coming to Laura's because there was always good food to eat.

The Dog House was big enough for a dog the size of an elephant. It was built by Laura's father and her oldest brother over fifteen years ago. Laura had two brothers and one sister, but they were

11

much older than she was. None of them lived at home.

It was called the Dog House because from the outside it looked like a giant doghouse with a door. Also, the name of the first club to use it was The Dogs.

Since then, it had been home to The Paul McCartney Fan Club, The Spiders, The Cowgirls, The Destroyers, The Erasers, The Devils, and now a new club: Pig City.

Laura was the president of Pig City. Allison said she should be mayor and not president because it was a city and not a country, but she was outvoted. Tiffany was vice-president and Allison was secretary. So far, they were the only members.

They entered the Dog House. Tiffany plopped down on a purple bean bag chair. Allison sat on a bed covered by a black-and-white checked bedspread. Laura sat in a swinging bamboo chair that hung from the ceiling.

There was also a bookcase, a television, two lamps, a coffee table, and various other odds and ends, mostly odds. Nearly everything came from garage sales.

Nothing electrical worked, which didn't matter since there were no electrical outlets. They had a battery-operated cassette tape recorder if they wanted to listen to music.

Laura made a fist with her right hand, then raised it and held it lengthwise against her nose, like a pig's snout. Allison and Tiffany did the same. Then they all solemnly lowered their fists. It was the secret Pig City salute.

Pig City was a secret club. It had to be. Clubs were no longer allowed at Laura's school. Earlier in the year there were several clubs, but a parent complained because her child couldn't join one. After that, clubs were no longer allowed.

"You're first, Allison," said Laura.

Allison blushed.

"What'd you bring, Allison?" asked Tiffany.

Allison removed a photograph from her jacket pocket and set it on the coffee table. "You don't have to stare at it!" she exclaimed.

It was a picture of her when she was three years old, naked in the bathtub.

"I got it out of my parents' album," she said. "Can you believe it? They used to show it to everyone who came over! I'd be sitting right there in the room with them, and they'd show the album to their friends, with that picture in it. 'How adorable,' they'd say. 'How precious.' Every one of my parents' friends has seen my butt!"

Tiffany laughed.

"Aw, how adorable," said Laura.

"It's not funny!" said Allison. She turned the picture over.

Laura had a jewelry box that looked just like an old-time pirate's treasure chest. She opened it and placed Allison's picture facedown on the torn red felt.

"Your turn, Tiffany," said Allison. "And it better be something good."

"It's better than yours," said Tiffany. "I mean worse."

Tiffany's lips were purple from the grape pop-

13

sicle. She unfolded what looked like the front page of a newspaper. A huge banner headline proclaimed:

### TIFFANY'S TICKLISH!

Allison and Laura laughed. Laura moved to the bed next to Allison, and they read it together.

*Tiffany, the world-famous spaghetti eater, is ticklish. That's right, ticklish! It has been conclusively established by our team of expert ticklers that she is ticklish all over.*

*A finger under her chin will cause her to giggle for hours. Squeeze her sides and she will jump six feet in the air. Touch a feather to her toes and watch her writhe on the floor in a fit of uncontrollable laughter. Tickle her armpits at your own risk!*

*Caution: Do not tickle her while she is eating spaghetti, or she will dump her plate on your head.*

"It's not funny!" said Tiffany. "Everybody who reads that stupid thing tries to tickle me."

"Where'd it come from?" Allison asked.

"Oh, my uncle had it made at a carnival we all went to. He wrote it himself, of course; it's so stupid."

"Did you really dump a plate of spaghetti on his head?" asked Laura.

"No!" Tiffany scowled. "That's another one of his so-called jokes that he thinks is funny. He always makes fun of me because of *one time* when we went to an Italian restaurant I got spaghetti sauce on my clothes. Of course, he thought it was hilarious.''

Laura got a peacock feather out of a blue vase on top of the bookcase. She held it menacingly over Tiffany, who was somewhat trapped in the bean bag chair.

Just the sight of the feather made Tiffany giggle. "Get away," she squealed.

Allison reached over and squeezed Tiffany's side. She jumped out of the chair.

Laura put the feather back in the vase and placed Tiffany's newspaper article in the treasure chest.

"Your turn, Laura," said Tiffany.

Laura took a folded piece of notebook paper out of the back pocket of her blue jeans and dropped it onto the coffee table. She returned to her swinging bamboo chair.

Allison unfolded Laura's paper. "Wow," she said, then handed it to Tiffany.

*Declaration of Love*
*I, Laura Sibbie, declare, now and forever,*
*that I'm in love with my teacher, Mr. Doyle. I*
*dream about him all the time, and if I was*
*older, I'd like to marry him.*
*With all my heart,*
*Laura Sibbie*

Tiffany gasped.

"Mr. Doyle?" asked Allison. "You're kidding!"

"I never lie," said Laura.

"I guess he's all right for a teacher," said Tiffany.

Laura placed her Declaration of Love in the treasure chest. She raised her fist to her nose. Tiffany and Allison did the same. Laura spoke. "If any one of us ever tells anybody anything about Pig City, the other two will show her secret to the whole school!"

They lowered their fists.

# 3
# Mr. Doyle

*Wednesday morning* Laura sneaked into the school building before school started. The main doors were locked, but she knew of a side door that would be open. She cautiously looked around, then walked boldly toward Mr. Doyle's room as if she had every right to be there.

Her school was once what was known as an "open school." There were no walls between the classrooms. But, in the last few years, the administration had done their best to "close" it.

Large wooden bookcases now separated one room from another. The door to Mr. Doyle's room was a yellow curtain hung between two metal closets. Laura pushed through.

Mr. Doyle wasn't there. She knew he wouldn't be. He was sitting at a table in the teacher's lounge drinking coffee and talking to the other teachers. That's where he was every morning. She sometimes fantasized about sitting there with him, drinking coffee and talking about interesting and important topics. She thought it sounded very romantic.

In the upper right-hand corner of the blackboard was the word DICTIONARY. Laura felt a pang of terror as she looked at that word. It was the most feared word in Mr. Doyle's class.

She picked up a piece of chalk and wrote in big letters in the center of the board:

PIGS RULE!

She set down the chalk, then walked back through the school and out the side door. Safe outside, she breathed a huge sigh of relief.

Someone tapped her shoulder.

She spun around.

"Oink, oink," said Gabriel.

She forced a smile.

Gabriel was a boy in her class. Ever since she started wearing her Pig City cap, he said, "Oink, oink," to her whenever he saw her.

She wondered if he had seen her come out of the building. She decided it didn't matter. Gabriel wouldn't tell on her. He never told on anyone, even though everybody was always telling on him.

Gabriel had copied more dictionary pages than anybody else in Mr. Doyle's class. That was Mr. Doyle's unique method of punishment. When kids got in trouble they had to copy a page out of the dictionary. They had to copy everything on the page, including the Latin origins and all the pro-nunciation symbols.

Laura hated the little upside-down e's the worst. She had copied fives pages over the year. She fig-ured Gabriel had probably copied a whole dictionary by now.

"Oink, oink," he said again.

She turned and walked away. Her hair swished around behind her, just missing his face.

Allison and Tiffany came across the blacktop. They raised their fists to their noses. Laura returned the salute.

They tried to decide whom else to ask to join Pig City. They finally settled on Kristin because she was smart. The problem was how to ask her while still keeping the club a secret.

Laura didn't tell them about her message on the board. She wanted it to be a surprise.

When the bell rang, they lined up and marched into class. Laura heard everybody ahead of her laugh at PIGS RULE! She laughed, too. If she hadn't, Mr. Doyle would have known she was the one who had written it. That was why he hadn't erased it yet. She knew how his mind worked. He wanted to see who didn't laugh.

You have to get up pretty early in the morning to try to outsmart me, Mr. Doyle, she thought.

He would have had to get up very early if he wanted to get up before Laura. Her alarm went off at 5:43. It took her an hour just to shampoo, comb, brush, and blow dry her hair.

"Laura, will you come up here, please," said Mr. Doyle.

She stood up, lifted her cap, shook her hair back,

and put the cap back on. She walked confidently to his desk.

"Do you know anything about this?" he asked.

She had to be careful not to tell a lie. She read aloud from the blackboard. " 'Pigs . . . Rule. . . .' What about it?"

"Why don't you tell me," said Mr. Doyle.

"How would I know?" she asked.

He smiled. "It's written on your hat."

Laura took off her cap and carefully studied the front of it. Then she looked at the board. "My hat doesn't say 'Pigs Rule,' Mr. Doyle. It says 'Pig City.' " She brushed her hair back off her face and put the cap back on.

He stared at her.

She smiled innocently back at him. She thought he was extremely handsome when he was being serious.

He was tall and very thin. He had a pale face with sunken cheeks and very cute, curly brown hair. She thought he looked like he read lots of good books.

"Do you know who wrote it?" he asked.

"It couldn't have been a pig," said Laura. "Pigs can't write."

"No, but sixth-grade girls can," he said.

"I know," said Laura. "We learned how to print in the first grade."

He told her to go back to her seat.

She turned around, swishing her hair behind her. She smiled at Tiffany and Allison. They were obviously very impressed. She raised her fist to her nose, then quickly lowered it. They did the same.

Her desk was on one side of the room, Tiffany's

was on the other side, and Allison was in the middle at the front. Mr. Doyle had learned at the beginning of the year to keep those three girls separated. She sat down.

"Linzy, will you erase the board, please," said Mr. Doyle.

Laura felt a little jealous as she watched Linzy erase the board. Linzy sat at the desk closest to Mr. Doyle and was always doing things for him. She was teacher's pet. She was the only person in the class who hadn't copied at least one dictionary page.

I wouldn't want to be teacher's pet, anyway, thought Laura. That's sickening. I can be in love with him without having to be his pet.

She put her hands behind her head, leaned back, and smiled contentedly.

# 4
# Kristin

*Outside at recess*, Allison and Tiffany were all excited. They thought PIGS RULE! was the greatest thing they'd ever seen.

"There's Kristin," said Allison.

Kristin was bent over, drinking from the water fountain. They walked up behind her.

"Hey!" Tiffany shouted.

Kristin jumped, and then had to cough out water that went down the wrong way. She turned around to face them.

She wore big red glasses that covered almost half of her mousy little face.

She was cute, but everyone thought she'd be cuter if she didn't have to wear glasses. Everyone was wrong. It was the glasses that made her look

so cute. Everyone also thought she was very intelligent. That wasn't true, either. It was her glasses
that made her look smart.

Tiffany, Laura, and Allison formed a semicircle
around her. She stood with her back against the
brick wall, next to the water fountain just outside
the library.

"We have a question to ask you," said Tiffany.

"Okay," said Kristin.

"Only we can't ask you the question," said Allison, "until we know your answer."

"How can I answer until I know the question?"
Kristin asked.

"You just have to answer yes or no," Allison
said.

"But you can't change your mind," said Tiffany.

"So what is it?" Laura demanded. "Yes or no?"

"What?" asked Kristin.

"Yes or no?" asked Tiffany.

"I have to know the question," Kristin insisted.

"Only if your answer is yes," said Allison. "If
your answer is no, then you'll never know the
question."

"Yes or no?" asked Tiffany.

"I don't know!"

"That's the same as no," said Laura.

"But I really don't know," said Kristin.

"Then it's no," Tiffany said coldly.

Kristin sighed.

The three girls turned their back on her and started
to walk away.

"Wait," said Kristin.

They turned around.

"Okay, yes."

"Good," said Laura. "Come to my house after school."

"But what's the question?" asked Kristin.

"We'll tell you at my house," said Laura. "Oh, and bring an extra pair of underpants with you."

Kristin had no choice. She had already said yes.

Gabriel was standing inside the library. He had to stay in during recess and help put books away because he had goofed off the day before during library period. He could see out through the tinted windows, but nobody on the outside could see in.

He could see Laura, Tiffany, Allison, and Kristin. He could hear everything they said. He watched Kristin walk away.

"Whew," said Tiffany.

"I thought she was going to say no for sure," said Allison.

Laura smiled. "Pig City must be kept secret," she said. "That's the most important thing."

They brought their fists to their noses.

So did Gabriel.

# 5
# Gabriel

*Mr. Doyle was in the middle* of teaching the class the difference between adjectives and adverbs. Gabriel understood the difference the first time it was explained.

He usually understood things the first time they were explained. That was one reason why he was always getting into trouble. He would get bored and have to find something else to do.

What is Pig City? he wondered. Why does Kristin have to bring an extra pair of underpants?

He looked at Laura. She sat three desks to the left of him. Her Pig City cap was pulled down tight over her long brown hair. He thought she had beautiful hair. He knew the story behind it, how she never told a lie. It made it even prettier to him. She was staring intently at Mr. Doyle, hanging on every word he said. Gabriel wished she would look at him like that someday.

If she asked me to answer yes or no, I'd say yes right away, he thought. I don't even care what the question is.

The problem was that whenever he tried to talk to her, his mind would go blank on him. He could never think of anything to say except for "Oink oink." It was stupid. He knew it was stupid, yet he said it, anyway.

He opened his desk and took out a piece of paper and a pencil.

*Dear Laura,* he wrote.

He chewed his eraser, then continued.

> *I know all about Pig City. Don't worry, I promise not to tell anybody.*

He smiled. He hoped it would trick her into telling him what Pig City was. Plus, she'd like him for not telling anybody. They could share the secret together.

> *You have very pretty hair.*
> > *Love,*
> > *Gabriel*

He read it over.

> *Dear Laura,*
> *I know all about Pig City. Don't worry, I promise not to tell anybody. You have very pretty hair.*
> > *Love,*
> > *Gabriel*

It was terrible. I practically told her I loved her! he thought.

The eraser on his pencil was chewed and wet, so he got a clean eraser from his desk.

First, he erased *Dear*. His father called his mother "dear." It was like calling her "darling" or "sweetie-pie." He wrote *Hey* in place of *Dear*. He erased the words *very pretty* and *love*, too.

He tried to think of what to write instead of *love*. He thought about "sincerely" or "yours truly," but didn't like either of those.

He wrote *Your humble servant*. He had seen it in a book once and thought it was funny. Laura will think it's funny, too, he thought. It will show her how clever I am.

He read it again.

*Hey Laura,*
   *I know all about Pig City. Don't worry, I promise not to tell anybody. You have a lot of hair.*
                    *Your humble servant,*
                    *Gabriel*

Much better.

He folded it into quarters and wrote Laura's name on the outside.

He waited until after school, until after Laura left the room, then put it in her desk.

# 6
# Sheila

*Sheila sat behind Gabriel.* She watched him write the note, although she couldn't see what it said. She watched him put it in Laura's desk.

She had guessed it would be for Laura. Gabriel was always staring at Laura. It made her sick.

She hated Laura. She hated her hair. She thought Laura was very conceited the way she swished it around when she walked, like she was a queen. She didn't believe that stuff about Laura never telling a lie, either.

Sheila had frizzy hair. She often lay awake at night and dreamed about setting Laura's hair on fire or sneaking into Laura's house and putting hair remover into her bottle of shampoo.

She waited for Gabriel to leave, then opened Laura's desk and removed the note.

*Hey Laura,*
*I know all about Pig City. Don't worry, I promise not to tell anybody. You have a lot of hair.*

*Your humble servant,*
*Gabriel*

Sheila's blood boiled. It was so obvious he was in love with Laura.

She was about to rip up the note, then stopped. She smiled. She looked through Laura's desk for a pencil with a good eraser. She thought a moment, then erased the whole second sentence. In its place she wrote:

*If you don't kiss me I will tell the whole school.*

She laughed. She erased *a lot of* and wrote *ugly*. When she finished, the note looked like this:

*Hey Laura,*
*I know all about Pig City. If you don't kiss me I will tell the whole school. You have      ugly      hair.*

*Your humble servant,*
*Gabriel*

She folded it back along the original folds and returned it to Laura's desk. Then she broke Laura's pencil.

# 7
# Insurance

*Laura, Allison, and Tiffany* sat on the front step of Laura's house, sucking root beer popsicles while they waited for Kristin.

"She should get contacts," said Allison. "She's cute, especially for a smart girl, but she'd look a lot better without those huge glasses of hers."

Tiffany agreed.

Laura didn't say anything. She had accidentally bitten off a large chunk of her popsicle, and it was freezing the roof of her mouth. She suffered in silent agony as she waited for the chunk to melt down small enough to swallow. For the moment, it was all she cared about. Her eyes watered.

Kristin pedaled her blue ten-speed bicycle to a stop on the sidewalk in front of them. She was out of breath.

Laura swallowed what was left of her frozen chunk of root beer. Her mouth slowly warmed. "Did you bring it?" she asked.

Kristin nodded. "In my backpack."

Tiffany looked around for a place to throw her popsicle stick, then finally stuck it in her shirt pocket. She walked behind Kristin and reached into her backpack with her sticky fingers. "Why'd you bring so many books?" she asked.

"Oh, you know Kristin," said Allison, "always reading."

Kristin hated to read. She brought the books because she needed something to cover up her underpants.

"Got 'em!" Tiffany exclaimed. She triumphantly held Kristin's underpants high in the air. They were white with a pink waistband.

"You don't have to show the whole world," said Kristin. Her face was almost as red as her glasses.

"Take them to the clubhouse," said Laura.

The four girls went through the gate to the backyard and on into the Dog House. There, Laura told Kristin the question that she had already answered: "Do you want to join Pig City?" She taught her the secret salute.

Kristin was greatly impressed.

"You can't tell anybody," Allison warned, "even if they torture you or threaten to kill you."

"I won't," Kristin promised.

"Your underpants are your insurance," said Laura. "If you tell anybody anything about Pig City, anything at all, we will take your underpants to school and show them to all the boys."

Kristin gasped. "I won't ever tell, never!" She

would rather have been tortured and killed than have her underpants shown to all the boys.

Tiffany got the treasure chest out from under the bed. Allison added Kristin's name to the list.

PIG CITY

*Laura — President*
*Tiffany — Vice-President*
*Allison — Secretary*
*Kristin — underpants*

Allison put the list and Kristin's underwear into the treasure chest, then Tiffany shoved it back under the bed.

They didn't show Kristin what they had each given as insurance. She wasn't allowed to know. There was a good reason for that. If Kristin broke her vow of secrecy, and they showed her underpants to the whole school, she might try to get revenge by telling everybody that Laura was in love with Mr. Doyle or Tiffany was ticklish or Allison liked to pose in the nude.

The four girls solemnly raised their fists to their noses.

"Welcome to Pig City," said Laura.

# 8
# Debbie

*Debbie was hanging upside-down* on the monkey bars. Laura, Allison, Tiffany, and Kristin looked upside-down to her.

There were still ten minutes before school started. There was going to be a math test first thing. Debbie always hung upside-down before tests. She said that all her blood went to her head and helped her think better.

They gave her the same choice they had given Kristin. "Yes or no?" asked Tiffany.

"Yes," Debbie answered right away. She was good at making quick decisions, especially when all her blood was in her head.

They told her to come to Laura's after school. "You forgot to tell her to bring an extra pair of underpants," said Kristin as they walked away.

"Everybody has to have a different kind of insurance," Laura explained.

"What will Debbie's be?" Kristin asked.

"You're not allowed to know," said Tiffany. "That's why everybody's has to be different."

"Don't worry," said Allison. "Laura will think of something good for Debbie."

Laura lifted her cap, shook her hair back, and put it back on.

The class lined up, then filed into Mr. Doyle's room. Everyone laughed. On the blackboard were the words:

PIGS ARE BEST!

Laura had sneaked in early again.

Mr. Doyle erased her message. He walked over to the side of the board and began to write something under the word DICTIONARY.

Immediately, everyone became very quiet. They waited to see whose name he'd put there. Whoever it was would have to stay after school and copy a dictionary page.

Laura wasn't worried. He can't possibly know it's me, not for sure.

Mr. Doyle stepped away from the board. Under the word DICTIONARY he had drawn a rectangle. Next to the rectangle he had written the number 2.

"When I find out who's been writing on the board," he said, "I will put his or *her* name inside the box." He looked directly at Laura. "That person will have to copy two dictionary pages; one for yesterday and one for today."

Laura smiled. You better make it three, she thought. There will be another one tomorrow.

Mr. Doyle told everyone to take out a pencil and paper for the math test. The class groaned. He handed a pile of tests to Linzy and asked her to please pass them out.

Laura opened her desk. She spotted the folded piece of paper with her name on it and smiled. She loved notes.

She made sure Mr. Doyle wasn't watching, then quickly unfolded it. Her smile disappeared.

*Hey Laura,*
   *I know all about Pig City. If you don't kiss me I will tell the whole school. You have     ugly     hair.*
                  *Your humble servant,*
                  *Gabriel*

She read it three times, then glanced at Gabriel.

He was looking at her and grinning from ear to ear. He touched his fist to his nose.

She looked away.

Linzy laid the math test on her desk.

Laura tried to stay calm. She knew Gabriel might still be watching her, so she didn't want to appear to be upset. She had to act like she was in control.

She saw her pencil had been broken. She wondered if Gabriel did that, too.

Since the test had already started, she couldn't ask to borrow another pencil from anyone. She used the broken one; one half for writing and one half for erasing.

The first question was a word problem: Question 1. *Count Dracula drank 7 gallons of blood every 2 weeks. How many quarts of blood did he drink a day?*

Mr. Doyle always tried to make his test questions interesting. Laura usually appreciated his cleverness. This time, however, she had more important things on her mind.

If he thinks I have ugly hair, why does he want to kiss me? And how does he know about Pig City? He can't. It's impossible! she fumed. Except she knew it wasn't impossible, because he had written the note. He knew the secret salute, too. Okay, she thought, he probably saw me come out of the building yesterday morning, so he knows I wrote on the board. He must have seen me give the salute, too. And my cap says "Pig City," so that's how he knows the name of the club. *Your humble servant???*

No matter what, she decided, there was no way she would kiss him! She hated him.

She tried to concentrate on the test. I wish somebody would drink Gabriel's blood — 2 gallons a day — until he shriveled up like a prune! She wrote "2 gallons" as the answer to the first problem.

She couldn't tell Tiffany or Allison about the note. She felt she was somehow to blame. If she was, then Allison and Tiffany would have to show her Declaration of Love to everybody in the school, including Mr. Doyle.

Question 2. *Mollie Morbid made many meatballs. From 1 lb. of meat she made nine meatballs. She had 4½ lbs. of meat. How many meatballs did Mollie Morbid make?*

But then if I don't kiss him, he'll tell everyone, and then Allison and Tiffany will show my Declaration of Love to Mr. Doyle, anyway. Pig City will be ruined, too. She shook her head. I can't do that to Allison or Tiffany or Kristin, especially after

36

the way we built it up to her. And what would we tell Debbie after school today? I have to kiss Gabriel. I have no choice.

Gabriel's a meatball! She divided 9 by 4½, and wrote 2 for her answer.

Except even if I kiss him, how do I know he still won't tell everybody about Pig City? He might tell everybody I kissed him, too.

Question 3. *3x + 15 = 39. What is the value for x?*

What if I tell him I'll kiss him only if he'll give insurance? She laughed.

"Do you find the test amusing, Laura?" asked Mr. Doyle.

She looked up. She knew Mr. Doyle thought she had laughed at one of his questions. Even though Mr. Doyle wrote humorous word problems, you weren't supposed to laugh at them. It was sort of a game between him and the class.

But she hadn't laughed at one of his questions. She had laughed at the thought of making Gabriel give her a pair of his underpants.

"I was just thinking," she said.

"That's good, Laura," said Mr. Doyle. "You should think when you are taking a test. It sometimes helps."

She returned to the test. She subtracted 15 from 39 and multiplied by 3. x = 72.

She had never kissed a boy before. She thought it was something she probably should do before next year. She didn't want to go to junior high inexperienced.

The thought of kissing Gabriel excited her a little bit. It also made her a little sick to her stomach.

# 9
# Laura's Reply

*Tiffany, Allison, and Laura* planned Debbie's insurance during lunch. Laura tried to look happy despite the sinking feeling in the pit of her stomach.

"Okay, how's this?" asked Tiffany. "We'll tell her she has to call a boy up on the phone. Then we can tape the phone conversation on Laura's tape recorder."

"That's good," said Allison. "And if Debbie tells anybody about Pig City, we'll play the tape for the whole class to hear. She'll have to tell the boy she loves him."

"Passionately," Tiffany said with great emotion. "She'll have to say she loves him *passionately*."

Allison laughed at the way Tiffany said that word.

"She'll have to disguise her voice," said Laura, trying to get in on the fun. "So the boy won't know who she is."

Tiffany and Allison continued to plan what Debbie would have to say to the boy, but Laura's mind was elsewhere. When she returned to class, she tore a piece of paper out of her notebook. Using her broken pencil, she wrote:

> *Hey Gabriel,*
> *I think you're uglier than a two-headed frog. I'll kiss you but only to save Pig City, not because I like you.*
> *Yours truly,*
> *Laura*
> *P.S. I'd rather kiss a rattlesnake!*

She gave up on the idea of asking him for insurance. He might make her give him insurance, instead. She'd just have to trust him. She frowned.

She folded the note in half, then in half again, then one more time. On the outside she wrote:

> *For Gabriel. Anybody else who reads this is a worm-nosed snail-eater.*

She passed it to the girl who sat next to her, who passed it to the boy next to her, who threw it at Gabriel.

It bounced off the side of his head and landed on the floor.

Gabriel grabbed for it.

"Gabriel!" said Mr. Doyle. "Bring that here."

"What?" asked Gabriel as he tried to hide it under his chair.

"You know what," said Mr. Doyle. "Bring the note here and write your name on the blackboard under 'Dictionary.'"

Gabriel picked up the note and slowly walked down the aisle to the front of the room. He read the outside, but didn't dare open it in front of the class.

Laura was slowly dying. Mr. Doyle usually read all notes out loud to the class. Don't read it, she prayed. Just throw it away. *Please.*

Mr. Doyle held out his hand. Gabriel dropped the note into it.

"Who's it from?"

Gabriel shrugged.

Mr. Doyle read the outside of the note, first to himself, then out loud. " 'For Gabriel. Anybody else who reads this is a worm-nosed snail-eater.' "

Everyone laughed.

"Maybe I better not read it," he joked.

"Read it! Read it!" chorused the class.

Don't. Please don't, Laura thought with all her might.

Mr. Doyle slowly began to unfold the note.

Laura stood up. "Don't read it, Mr. Doyle," she said. "I wrote it. Please don't read it."

"Laura, I'm surprised at you," said Mr. Doyle. "You know you're not supposed to pass notes in class."

"I know. Please don't read it."

"Read it!" shouted Sheila.

Mr. Doyle looked at the note, still folded in half. "Come here, Laura," he said.

She walked to the front of the room next to Gabriel.

"All right," said Mr. Doyle. "I won't read it." He gave her back the note.

"Oh, thank you, Mr. Doyle!" she said. "Thank you very much!"

"You read it," he said.

She turned white.

"Read it aloud to the class," he told her. "If you can say it to Gabriel, then you can say it to everyone."

She swallowed, then slowly turned and faced the class. Her legs wobbled beneath her. She looked at Allison's sympathetic face in the front row.

"We're waiting," said Mr. Doyle.

She took a deep breath. She couldn't believe this was happening. She lifted her cap, brushed her hair off her face, and put the cap back on. She didn't say a word.

"Throw it away," said Mr. Doyle.

She didn't have to be told twice. She tore the note to shreds and dropped it in the trash.

"Let this be a lesson," said Mr. Doyle. "Never put anything in a letter that you wouldn't want published on the front page of a newspaper. A word to the wise. Now go write your name on the board."

Laura gladly wrote her name on the blackboard under the word DICTIONARY, under the rectangle.

"You, too, Gabriel," said Mr. Doyle.

"Why me?" he protested. "I didn't write it. I didn't even get to read it."

Several kids laughed.

Mr. Doyle glared at him.

He walked behind Laura and waited for her to finish writing her name.

Their fingers touched as she handed him the piece of chalk.

# 10
# Maybe. Maybe Not.

*School was almost over,* and the tips of Gabriel's fingers still tingled. For the first time in his life he was looking forward to copying a dictionary page. Laura would be there, too. He would have given anything to know what was in her note.

Maybe she'll tell me, he hoped. Maybe she'll tell me all about Pig City. Maybe she likes me. Please maybe. . . . His mind ran wild with maybes.

Laura looked at the clock. In five minutes she'd be alone with Gabriel. She'd have to say yes to his face. No more notes.

Mr. Doyle never stayed after with kids when they had to copy dictionary pages. "Why should *I* have to stay after school because *you* got in trouble?"

he always said. "I have better things to do than play nursemaid to you."

Laura knew that, in his own way, Mr. Doyle was really saying, "Even though you got in trouble, I still trust you enough to leave you alone in the room." Normally, she liked that. Not today. She was afraid Gabriel would try to kiss her in the classroom.

When the final bell rang, her friends crowded around her desk.

"Wha'd the note say?" asked Tiffany.

They were all dying to know.

"I told him I thought he was uglier than a two-headed frog," she told them. It wasn't a lie.

Allison laughed.

"What's wrong with *that*?" asked Tiffany. "I would have read that out loud."

"I don't think Gabriel's ugly," said Kristin. "He's cute."

"I hate him," said Laura.

"Do you girls want to copy dictionary pages, too?" asked Mr. Doyle.

"No," said Allison.

They turned to go. "We won't tell Debbie anything until you get there," Allison told Laura. Mr. Doyle followed them out through the yellow curtain.

Laura watched Gabriel get up from his desk and walk to the metal closet. That was where Mr. Doyle kept the dictionaries. He had about fifty old paperback dictionaries. They were used just for punishment. There was a large hardcover dictionary that was used for normal dictionary purposes.

She watched Gabriel thumb through a dictionary, obviously waiting for her. I'm not going to kiss him here in school, she thought. I'll do it in the Dog House.

She stood up, lifted her cap, wiped her hair back, and pulled the cap back down. She walked up beside him and grabbed one of the paperback dictionaries.

"Pick a page with a picture," he said.

She nearly jumped out of her skin. "What?"

"Pick a picture page," he repeated. "If you pick a page with a picture, then you won't have to copy as much. You don't have to copy the picture."

She looked at him as though he were crazy. "Have you told anyone about Pig City?" she asked.

"No. I told you I wouldn't."

"Yes, I know what you told me," said Laura.

"I meant it," said Gabriel. He smiled.

She couldn't bear to look at his smiling face. She detested him. "Okay," she said firmly. "But not here in school. Can you come over to my house after dinner?"

"Sure!"

"Okay, then," said Laura.

"Okay," said Gabriel. He tore a page with a picture out of his dictionary and returned with it to his seat. *Maybe!*

Laura ripped a page out of her dictionary. She brought it back to her desk and slowly and carefully copied everything on it, still using her broken pencil.

A half an hour later, she looked up to see Gabriel drop his completed pages on Mr. Doyle's desk. "You're through?" she asked hatefully. She was only a little more than halfway done with hers.

"Sure," he said with a shrug. He walked back to her desk and watched her write. "You should have picked a page with a picture."

She ignored him.

"You're writing too neatly, also. You should write fast and sloppy. You'll get done quicker, and it makes it harder for Mr. Doyle to see if you made any mistakes." He was an expert at copying dictionary pages.

Laura continued to write at her own pace.

"Well, see you later."

She cringed.

When she finally finished, she had used both sides of two pieces of notebook paper plus half a side of another page. She stapled it to the dictionary page and put it on Mr. Doyle's desk.

On the blackboard, she wrote:

PIGS FLY HIGH!

# 11
# Howard

*When Laura got home,* she found Tiffany, Allison, and Debbie waiting inside her house in the kitchen. They were eating licorice sticks and finishing off the last of the frozen pepperoni pizza that Laura's mother had microwaved for them. Each girl had a glass of grape juice in front of her.

They all said, "Hi." Tiffany and Allison didn't salute, not with Debbie there.

Allison went to the Dog House and got the tape recorder.

Tiffany went into the living room to get more licorice. It was kept in a jar on the coffee table. The first time she came over to Laura's house, she couldn't believe she could take as much as she wanted. "You mean I don't even have to ask your mother? She won't care?" She had never heard of such a thing.

They started down the hall toward Laura's room. Pictures of Laura's family, from her great-grandparents to her nephew, lined the walls.

"Laura, you're home," her mother said, going the other way. "What happened?"

"I had some work to do for Mr. Doyle," she explained. "I needed to use the dictionary."

She led her friends into her room and closed the door. She had her own phone, with her own private number. She took the phone off the top of her dresser and placed it on the thickly carpeted floor. Everyone sat around it. Allison got the tape recorder ready.

"Before we tell you anything," said Laura, "we need insurance."

"What kind of insurance?"

"You have to call up a boy in our class and tell him that you're secretly in love with him," said Allison.

"Passionately," said Tiffany.

"We'll tape the whole thing," said Laura. "Then if you tell anybody our secret, we'll play the tape in front of Mr. Doyle's class."

"What secret?"

"We'll tell you after you call up the boy."

"Disguise your voice, and don't tell him who you are," said Tiffany. "He'll never know, unless you break your vow of secrecy."

"What boy?" asked Debbie.

Laura looked at Tiffany and Allison. They hadn't picked the boy.

"How about Gabriel?" suggested Allison.

"No!" Laura shouted.

Tiffany and Allison looked at her strangely.

"Okay, who?" asked Debbie.

"How about Howard?" Laura suggested.

Everyone laughed.

It was because of Howard that clubs were no longer allowed at school. Howard's mother had called and complained that none of the clubs would let Howard join.

Tiffany looked up Howard's number in the phone book and called it out. Debbie pushed the buttons on Laura's phone. Allison turned on the tape recorder. She held the microphone next to Debbie's mouth.

"Hello," Debbie said in a husky whisper. "May I talk to Howard, please?"

She turned to the others. "I think that was his mother."

They laughed.

"Howard?" said Debbie. She hammed it up. "Oh, Howard, is it really you? This is . . . your secret admirer. I love you, Howard. You're so handsome."

"Passionately," Tiffany whispered.

"I love you passionately," Debbie said with feeling.

"Who is this?" asked Howard.

"I can't tell you," said Debbie. "I'm afraid you'll break my heart." She hung up.

Everyone laughed.

Allison spoke into the microphone. "That was Debbie. She just called Howard and told him she loved him passionately, didn't you, Debbie?" She handed her the microphone.

"Yes," said Debbie. "That was me. I'm Debbie. I disguised my voice because I love Howard so much, and I'm afraid he won't love me back."

They all laughed. Allison switched off the tape recorder.

"Welcome to Pig City," said Laura, fist at nose.

# 12
# The Kiss

"*So, tell us about* school today," said Laura's mother during dinner. "Anything special happen?"

Laura nearly swallowed her piece of pot roast whole. She coughed, then pointed to her mouth. She chewed her meat very slowly as she tried to think of something that happened — something she could tell her parents. She swallowed and took a drink of water.

"We had a math test," she said.

"Oh, how'd you do?" asked her father.

She shrugged. She knew she'd be lucky just to have passed it. She had only answered fourteen questions out of twenty. "Mr. Doyle hasn't graded it yet," she said. "It doesn't matter, anyway."

"What do you mean it doesn't matter?" asked her father.

"We've been having tests all year," Laura explained. "One more test isn't going to make too much of a difference." Right after she said that, she knew it was a mistake.

Her parents gave her a long lecture about how every test, every homework assignment, is important. She must never let up. Just because her grades had been good so far, that was no reason to quit. They compared it to a race. It doesn't matter how far in front you are; if you stop before you reach the finish line, you won't win.

Laura said "yes," or "I know," or "you're right," at least a dozen times during the conversation, though she was hardly listening. Her mind was on Gabriel.

She decided she'd get it over with quickly. When Gabriel arrived, she would step outside, kiss him, tell him she hated his guts, then step inside and close the door. One, two, three, that was the way to do it. It was always best to do dreadful things quickly, and then be done with them.

"If you form good study habits now, while you're young, they'll stick with you for the rest of your life," said her father.

"That's good advice," said Laura. "I'll remember that."

"Your father's right," said her mother. "When I was your age, I didn't have to study and I got good grades. But when I went to college I had trouble because I had never learned *how* to study. It's the students with good study habits, not necessarily the smart ones, who succeed in college."

"You're right," said Laura. "May I be excused?"

"You've hardly touched your dinner," said her father.

"I guess I'm not hungry," she said. She was too nervous to eat.

"All right," said her mother, "but don't come back in an hour and expect me to feed you."

Laura left the table. She went to the bathroom, where she brushed her teeth and rinsed her mouth with mouthwash. Even though she hated Gabriel, she didn't want to have bad breath when she kissed him.

She waited nervously in her room, listening for the doorbell. She had to be sure she answered it before her parents. When her phone rang she jumped. She started to answer it, but stopped. She didn't want to be on the phone talking to Tiffany or Allison when the doorbell rang. The phone kept ringing. She'd have to make it quick. She picked up the receiver. "Hello!"

"Hello, Laura, this is Gabriel."

She collected herself. "Where are you?"

"Home," he said sadly. "I can't come over tonight. I'm grounded because I had to copy another dictionary page. I have to stay home all weekend, too."

"Gee, that's tight," said Laura. She wondered how it would affect their deal.

"I told my parents they could ground me for two months if they'd just let me out *tonight*, but they said no."

Laura felt flattered. She got an idea. She lay back

on her bed. "How would you like to join Pig City?" she asked.

"Sure!" he replied.

"Of course, you know that means you'd have to give insurance."

"Of course," said Gabriel.

She could hardly believe how well this was working out. "You understand," she asked, "that if I let you join Pig City, then I don't have to, um, do anything else?"

"I understand."

"Okay, when do you get off being grounded?"

"Next week. Monday."

"Okay, after school on Monday."

"All right."

"Good, then it's all set," said Laura. "In the meantime, don't tell anyone."

"I won't. I promise."

They said good-bye and hung up.

Laura was amazed. It was perfect. There was no reason not to let him join, since he already knew all about Pig City, anyway. And she didn't have to kiss him anymore.

She felt a little disappointed, however, that he had so quickly dropped his demand to kiss her, just to join Pig City.

She walked back down the hall to the kitchen. Her parents were just putting the last of the dishes in the dishwasher.

"I'm hungry," she said. "Is there anything to eat?" She sat down at the table.

As she ate the leftover dinner, she tried to think of different possible insurances for Gabriel.

# 13
# Karen and Yolanda

*Everyone laughed* when they saw PIGS FLY HIGH on the blackboard. Mr. Doyle didn't say a word. He merely erased it and put the number 3 next to the rectangle under the word DICTIONARY.

He had told the class earlier in the year that anybody who didn't complete all of his or her dictionary pages by the end of the year wouldn't graduate. Laura wasn't worried. She didn't think he really would keep somebody from graduating just for that. Besides, it was only three. Besides, he had to catch her first.

She had a bigger problem. Somehow, she had to convince Allison and Tiffany to let Gabriel join Pig City. Last night it had seemed the perfect solution to her problem. Now, it seemed almost impossible. Maybe it would be easier just to kiss him, she thought.

Mr. Doyle handed back the math tests. He had them arranged in order from worst to best. Laura's was on the top.

"What happened, Laura?" he asked as he placed her test on her desk. "That isn't like you."

She saw a red D-plus at the top of the page. "I guess I had a bad day," she said.

"I'd say so. I'd hate to see you fall apart now, after you've been doing so well all year."

Laura shrugged. Mr. Doyle continued passing back the tests. One test won't matter, she thought.

"So who should we ask to join today?" Tiffany asked as the three girls walked out to recess.

Laura scrunched up her face. She wondered what they'd say if she suggested Gabriel. No, she didn't wonder. She knew. That was the problem.

"How about Karen?" said Allison. "She's fun."

"No," Laura said. "Karen's always talking. How do we know if we can trust her, even with insurance?"

Allison and Tiffany agreed. Karen talked too much. She was too happy, too. They couldn't trust someone who smiled all the time.

"What about Yolanda?" said Tiffany. "She never says anything!"

"I like Yolanda a lot," said Allison. "She's nice."

Laura tried to think of something wrong with Yolanda.

Debbie and Kristin joined them. Five fists met five noses.

"Who are we going to get today?" asked Kristin.

"And what are we going to do to her?" asked Debbie.

"Yolanda," said Tiffany. "Only you're not allowed to know what she does for her insurance."

"That's not fair!" complained Debbie.

"Do you want her to know what you did for insurance?" Allison asked.

"No!" said Debbie.

"Well, then?" said Tiffany.

"Is Yolanda all right with you, Laura?" Allison asked.

"I guess so."

The citizens of Pig City searched for Yolanda.

They found her sitting with Karen on the edge of a planter. Yolanda and Karen were best friends. Karen liked to talk and Yolanda liked to listen.

"We have to talk to Yolanda alone," said Tiffany.

Karen got up and left. She didn't mind. Nothing ever bothered Karen, not even Gabriel.

Karen sat in front of Gabriel in Mr. Doyle's class, so she was often the victim of his pranks. Once, he tied her shoelaces to her chair. When she tried to stand up, she fell over and her desk rolled on top of her. She twisted her ankle. She didn't mind.

Gabriel kept saying how sorry he was, but she just laughed. Yolanda and Sheila had to carry her to the nurse's office. She talked and made jokes the whole way.

Yolanda was the opposite of Karen. She was very shy and hardly ever said anything. She was scared to death of boys. She was very pretty, too. She had golden skin and jet black hair, but her shyness kept her from being popular.

They told her to come to Laura's house after school.

She said she would.

They told her not to tell anyone.

She said she wouldn't.

It was too easy. Yolanda was too nice and too scared to say no.

As they walked away from her, Laura saw Gabriel leaning against the school building watching them. His fist was on his nose. She looked around at her friends, but they didn't seem to notice him.

"I have to go to the bathroom," she said. She went to the bathroom, so it wouldn't be a lie. She went in, turned around, and went out. Then she went to Gabriel.

"So, when do I join Pig City?" he asked.

"You're not allowed to do that," she told him.

"Do what?"

"The Pig City salute. You're not allowed to touch your nose until you become an official member."

"You changed your mind, didn't you? I knew it!"

"Be cool," she said. "Just don't salute anymore. Everything will work out." She turned and walked away. Her hair swished around behind her.

It was Friday. Gabriel got off being grounded on Monday. She had until then to either figure out some way to let him join or kiss him.

# 14
# Jonathan

*After school*, Laura, Allison, and Tiffany waited in front of Laura's house for Yolanda. They thought up the perfect insurance for her. She'd have to write a love note to a boy. Then if she told anybody about Pig City, they'd put the note in the boy's desk. She was so scared of boys, she'd die before she told anyone.

"We'll let her pick the boy," said Laura.

"She won't be able to," said Allison. "She's too shy."

"We'll make her pick one," said Tiffany.

"I bet she can't do it," said Allison. "I bet she can't even say a boy's name."

When Yolanda arrived, they tied a dish towel over her eyes, then led her around to the Dog House. They sat her down on the bed. Laura told her what she had to do for insurance.

"And *you* have to pick the boy," said Tiffany.

"Okay," said Yolanda. "Jonathan."

They were shocked.

Allison untied the blindfold. Yolanda blinked her baby blue eyes as she looked around the clubhouse. They gave her a piece of paper and a pen.

Tiffany dictated: "Dearest Darling Jonathan. . . ."

Yolanda blushed as she wrote down everything Tiffany said.

Laura didn't especially like Jonathan, but she knew a lot of girls thought he was handsome. Laura didn't like boys with blond hair. Jonathan's hair was so blond that in the summer, when he went swimming, the chlorine from swimming pools gave it a green tint. Besides being handsome, Jonathan was also probably the smartest boy in Mr. Doyle's class and also the best athlete. He knew it, too. That was the main reason Laura didn't like him. She thought he was too conceited.

Gabriel is smarter than Jonathan, she thought, even if his grades aren't as good.

Yolanda finished writing the note. It read:

> *Dearest Darling Jonathan,*
> *I'm madly in love with you. I dream about kissing you all the time. You're so handsome. I'd love to run my fingers through your hair.*
> *Love,*
> *Yolanda*

# 15
# Executive Session

*Over the weekend*, Laura, Tiffany, and Allison met in the Dog House to discuss the future of Pig City. They ate pickles and chocolate chip cookies and drank lime slushes.

"Who else do we want to join?" Tiffany asked. She took a large bite out of a kosher dill pickle.

"I think we have enough members for now," said Allison. "Let's do something spectacular!"

"Like what?" asked Tiffany.

"We could have a bake sale," Allison suggested.

"Ooh! How spectacular!" Tiffany said sarcastically.

"We could raise money with a bake sale," Allison explained, "and *then* do something spectacular."

"We're a secret club," said Tiffany. "If we have a bake sale, then everybody will know about us."

"Oh, yeah," said Allison.

Tiffany took another bite of pickle. "Unless we sell invisible cakes," she said.

Allison laughed, even though the joke was mostly on her.

"I think we should ask boys to join Pig City," said Laura.

Tiffany dropped her pickle.

The three girls watched it roll across the floor and under the television.

Allison said, "Um, well, who do you have in mind, Laura?"

Laura didn't want to play her hand too quickly. "We should ask three boys," she said. "We should each pick one."

Allison looked down at the floor. Tiffany stared up at the ceiling.

"We made Yolanda pick a boy," said Laura. "If she can do it, why can't we?"

Tiffany and Allison remained silent.

"They'll have to give insurance," said Laura, "just like everybody else."

That was the clincher. Smiles formed on the faces of her two best friends.

"Who picks first?" asked Tiffany.

"You can, if you want," said Allison.

"I didn't say I wanted to," said Tiffany.

"Well, do you?" asked Laura.

"I don't know," said Tiffany.

"Go ahead, Tiffany," said Allison. "Who do you pick?"

Tiffany started to giggle.

"If you don't choose," said Laura, "Allison or I might pick the boy you want."

Tiffany stopped giggling. A glow came to her cheeks and there was a sparkle in her eyes. "Nathan," she said sweetly.

Laura and Allison laughed.

"What's so funny about Nathan!" Tiffany demanded.

"Nothing," said Laura. "It was just the way you said it."

"I just said, 'Nathan,' " said Tiffany.

They laughed again. Tiffany laughed, too.

"Okee-dokee-do!" said Allison.

Okee-dokee-do was one of Nathan's favorite expressions.

"Your turn, Allison," Tiffany said sharply. "Who do you choose?"

"Oh, I don't know," said Allison. "I can't think of any boy I especially like."

"How about Carl?" suggested Tiffany.

"No. I don't know," said Allison.

"How about Aaron?" asked Laura knowingly.

Allison blushed. "Aaron? It doesn't matter to me. Okay, Aaron."

"How about Jonathan?" suggested Tiffany.

"No," said Allison, "Yolanda wrote Jonathan a note. I guess Aaron will be okay."

"How about Paul?" suggested Tiffany.

"I said 'Aaron!' " Allison snapped at her.

Tiffany's mouth dropped open. She covered it with the palm of her hand and stared at Allison, wide-eyed. She took her hand away and said, "You like Aaron, don't you?"

62

Allison shrugged. "He's okay. He dresses nice."

Laura and Tiffany broke up laughing. "His grandmother picks out his clothes!" said Tiffany.

"Your turn, Laura," Allison said brusquely.

"Who do you pick, Laura?" asked Tiffany.

Laura lifted her cap off her head, brushed her hair off her face, and put the cap back on. "Gabriel."

Tiffany and Allison were too stunned to laugh.

"I thought you hated Gabriel," said Allison.

"I think Gabriel will be a loyal citizen of Pig City," Laura asserted.

"You said he looked like a two-headed frog," said Tiffany.

"So," said Laura, "maybe I like two-headed frogs."

Her friends laughed.

"Aaron's got nice eyes," Allison said sweetly.

"Nathan's as cute as a bug," said Tiffany.

# 16
# Insurance for Boys

*It wasn't easy* trying to think up insurance for boys. They couldn't ask a boy to give them a pair of his underpants. They didn't want to ask a boy they liked to call up another girl and tell her he loved her.

These were some other ideas they thought up, then rejected for obvious reasons:

Paint nail polish on their toenails. Then, we'll take off their shoes if they tell anybody about Pig City. (Tiffany)

Tell them to buy baby dolls at the toy store. Then show the dolls to everyone if they tell anyone about Pig City. (Laura)

Make them give us all their socks. Then we'll meet them before school every day and give them their pair of socks for the day. If they tell anybody about Pig City, we'll give them socks that don't match! (Allison)

Make them drink poison. They have to drink the antidote every day for the rest of their lives or else they'll die. We'll be the only ones who have the antidote. If they tell anybody about Pig City, they die! It doesn't really have to be poison. We can make it ourselves using prune juice, vanilla, and food coloring. They might think that it's not really poison, but they wouldn't know for sure. Instead of saying it's poison, we can tell them it's a magic love potion. If they don't take the antidote every day, they'll fall in love with every girl they see, including dogs and cats. (All three)

Make them cut up onions until they cry. Then we'll save their tears and show them to everyone if they tell anybody about Pig City, and everyone will call them crybabies. (Laura)

Make them call up a pizza parlor and order twenty large pizzas but not give their name and address. Then if they tell anybody about Pig City, we'll call the pizza parlor back and tell them where to send the pizzas. (Tiffany)

"With lots of anchovies," she added.

"That's the dumbest idea you've had yet," said Allison.

All three girls lay on the floor. Tiffany had one foot in the bean bag chair. The lime slushes, cookies, and pickles were long gone.

"We can make them put on funny clothes," said Laura, "and then take their picture. My sister left a lot of old clothes at our house. We could make them wear a dress!"

"No, that wouldn't work for Aaron," said Tiffany. "He already dresses funny." She and Laura laughed.

Allison didn't. "Just because Aaron doesn't dress like everybody else — " she said. "There's no law saying you have to wear blue jeans and sneakers! I think Aaron dresses like a perfect gentleman."

"I think he dresses like a perfect nerd," said Tiffany.

"Okay, I have another idea," Laura said after a while. "We can make a tape of each boy saying something stupid. Then, if they tell, we'll play the tape to the school."

"No, that wouldn't work for Nathan," said Allison. "He always says stupid things." She and Laura laughed.

Tiffany didn't. "Nathan says a lot of very intelligent things," she said. "It's just that everybody else is too dumb to understand them."

"Name one smart thing he's said," said Allison.

Tiffany thought a moment. "Hey, half a pickle," she said. She found the rest of her pickle, which had rolled under the television.

"I have an idea," said Allison. "We can make them write a nasty letter to Mr. Doyle. Then, if they tell anybody about Pig City, we'll give the letter to Mr. Doyle. They'd have to stay after school and copy a dictionary page."

"No, that won't work for Gabriel," said Tiffany. "He's always copying dictionary pages." She and Allison laughed.

Laura didn't. "It's not always his fault," she said. "Everybody always tells on him. He never tells on anybody."

"How about this?" said Tiffany. "I have the best idea yet." She smiled mysteriously.

"What?" asked Allison.

"How about this? Before they can join Pig City, we tell them they have to kiss us!"

Laura and Allison looked uncertainly at each other. "How will that work for insurance?" Laura asked.

Tiffany shrugged. "I don't know."

This time they all laughed.

# 17
# Arrangements

*Laura wrote* PIGMENTATION on the blackboard. It was the biggest "pig" word she could find. She had looked through the large hardcover dictionary. She knew she had time because Mr. Doyle was usually a little slow on Monday mornings. He often came late to class, bringing his cup of coffee with him. Laura imagined that was due to wild weekends spent with beautiful and exotic women.

She erased the number 3 next to the rectangle under the word DICTIONARY. She wrote the number 4 in its place. That'll show him how much he scares me!

Mr. Doyle walked in a couple of minutes late, carrying his cup of coffee. He went straight to the blackboard and erased PIGMENTATION. He walked over to DICTIONARY. When he saw the number had already been changed, he was so surprised it made him drop the chalk. It landed plop into his cup of coffee.

The class was hysterical.

"Okay, settle down," he said. He pulled out the wet piece of chalk. "How do you take your coffee?" he asked. "Cream and chalk," he answered.

Everyone laughed again.

Mr. Doyle looked at his cup of coffee as if he was wondering if he could still drink it. "I guess I better start getting here earlier," he said, glancing up at Laura.

She smiled at him.

She and her friends had finally decided on insurance for the boys. Aaron would have to sing a silly song into the tape recorder. Nathan would have to write a nasty letter to Mr. Doyle. Gabriel would have his picture taken wearing one of Laura's sister's old dresses.

They had quickly rejected the idea of kissing them. For one thing, it wouldn't work for insurance. For another, none of them had the guts to say it to the boys.

At recess, they split up. Allison went to find Aaron. Tiffany went after Nathan.

Laura spoke with Gabriel.

He started to salute, then stopped, remembering what she had told him. "Am I in?" he asked eagerly.

"Ssh! Not so loud," she cautioned.

He waited.

She took off her cap, wiped her hair off her face, then put the cap back on. "You have to give insurance first."

"Right, I knew that," he said.

She told him to come to her house after dinner. She knew Aaron and Nathan were supposed to come right after school.

She met up with Tiffany and Allison. They were both very excited.

"Boys are so dumb," said Tiffany. "They'll do anything you tell them!"

"I told Aaron to come to your house and we'd tell him what pigmentation meant," said Allison. "He said he already knew what it meant — color. I told him that was only the dictionary definition. I said I'd teach him the *real* meaning."

"I didn't tell Nathan nothing," said Tiffany. "I asked him yes or no? and he said, 'Okee-dokee-do.' "

The three girls laughed.

"What about you, Laura?" asked Allison. "Is Gabriel coming?"

"Oh, I found out he was grounded," Laura said. "I guess I'll talk to him tomorrow."

Nothing she said was a lie. He had been grounded, and she probably would talk to him tomorrow.

She didn't want Tiffany and Allison there when Gabriel was initiated. She was afraid they might find out he already knew all about Pig City.

"I hope they'll agree to give insurance," said Allison.

"Boys are so dumb," said Tiffany. "They'll do anything we tell 'em."

# 18
# Nathan and Aaron

*After school,* the Pig City executives waited at Laura's house for Aaron and Nathan. They were so nervous, they laughed at anything anybody said. They laughed when Laura's mother asked them if they would like a frozen pizza.

"Of course, I'll heat it up first," she explained.

That made them laugh harder.

She shrugged. "I should be a comedian."

"We don't want any pizza," said Laura.

"Thank you, anyway," said Allison.

"Yeah, thanks," said Tiffany, then she cracked up again.

When the doorbell rang, the laughter ceased.

They all got up to answer it.

Nathan and Aaron stood on the other side of the door.

"Hi," said Nathan.

"Hi," said Allison.

"Hi," said Laura.

"Hi," said Aaron.

"Hi," said Tiffany.

"Hi," Nathan said again.

"C'mon, let's go," said Laura. She, Tiffany, and Allison stepped outside. Aaron and Nathan stepped inside. They crashed in the middle.

"This way," said Laura. She led them around the side of the house to the backyard, then into the clubhouse. Nathan was first. They told Aaron to wait outside.

"Wowie zowie," said Nathan as he looked around the Dog House. He sat on the bed.

Tiffany sat next to him. Her right leg and Nathan's left leg were less than an inch apart. Laura sat in the swinging chair, and Allison was on the giant purple bean bag.

"We're about to tell you a secret," said Laura. "You must never repeat any of it to anybody."

"I won't," he said. "Cross my liver." He made an X over his left side where his liver was, or at least where Laura thought it was. She didn't know for sure.

"We need insurance," said Allison.

"You mean like life insurance?"

"You have to write a nasty letter to Mr. Doyle," said Tiffany. "We'll tell you what you have to write."

"Then, if you break your vow of secrecy," said Allison, "we'll give him your letter."

"Hey, that's neat," said Nathan. "That's clever."

They gave him a piece of paper and a pen. He

leaned over and wrote on the top of the coffee table as the three girls dictated to him.

"Dear Mr. Doyle," Allison began.

*Dear Mr. Doyle*, wrote Nathan.

"You stink," said Laura.

*You stink*, he wrote.

They made it up as they went along.

"You are the most ugliest teacher in the school!" said Tiffany.

"You're too stupid to be a teacher!" said Laura.

"And you have bad breath," said Allison.

"Wait, not so fast," said Nathan, as he furiously tried to keep up. " 'Have bad breath.' Go on."

"I hate you," said Laura. She waited for him to finish. "Then sign it, 'Sincerely, Nathan.' "

Nathan finished the letter. Laura read it over, then gave it to Allison. She put it in the treasure chest.

Nathan's and Tiffany's legs were now touching, but they each pretended not to notice.

"Welcome to Pig City," said Laura, nose and fist together.

Nathan returned the salute. "I'm proud to be a member of such a fine organization," he said.

Aaron was next.

Between the time Nathan left and Aaron entered, Tiffany and Allison switched positions. Allison was on the bed. Tiffany was on the beans.

Aaron sat next to Allison. He wore brown slacks and hard shoes. His shirt looked freshly ironed. His hair was neatly combed. You could tell just by looking at Aaron that he always wore clean underwear, too.

73

"I thought clubs were illegal," he said.

"What club?" asked Allison.

"I don't know anything about a club," said Tiffany.

Aaron smiled. "I don't know anything about a club, either."

Allison smiled at him.

For his insurance, he had to sing a song into the tape recorder.

It had three verses. Each girl had written a different verse. Allison handed him a piece of paper with all the words. "You have to sing this," she said. "Then if you tell anybody what we tell you, we'll play the tape for the whole school, over the PA system."

"It's to the tune of 'Mary Had a Little Lamb,' " said Tiffany.

Aaron looked it over. "Okay, I'm ready," he said. He put the paper down. He had it memorized.

Laura handed Aaron the microphone, turned her cassette player to record, and signaled for him to start.

He sang:


*"I am such a stupid jerk,*
*Stupid jerk, stupid jerk,*
*I am such a stupid jerk,*
*I don't have a brain."*


That verse was written by Laura. She didn't dare look at Tiffany. If she did, she knew they'd both crack up.

Allison listened serenely to Aaron's serenade.

> *"I just love to pick my nose,*
> *Pick my nose, pick my nose,*
> *I just love to pick my nose,*
> *It is so much fun."*

That was Tiffany's verse. The last one was Allison's.

> *"I'm in love with every girl,*
> *Every girl, every girl,*
> *I'm in love with every girl,*
> *In Mr. Doyle's class."*

Laura turned off the recorder. Allison clapped her hands.

# 19
# A Dress for Gabriel

*Laura quickly gobbled down* her dinner, hardly pausing for a breath of air. "May I be excused?" she asked.

"We don't have a daughter," said her father. "We have a vacuum cleaner."

Laura laughed.

"You know, you really shouldn't eat so fast," said her mother. "It's not good for the digestion."

"Too late now," said Laura.

"You may be excused," her father told her.

She rinsed off her plate in the sink, then stuck it in the dishwasher. She hurried to the back of the house to get ready for Gabriel. She went into her sister's old room.

When her sister had moved into her own apartment, she left a lot of old clothes behind. Most of them were pretty tacky. Laura thought they'd be perfect for Gabriel.

She rummaged through the dresses hanging in the closet. She took out a frilly white one and held it up in front of her, trying to imagine how it would look on Gabriel. She shook her head.

She stuck her head back in the closet, then gasped with delight. She saw the perfect dress for Gabriel.

It was a Hawaiian muumuu. It was bright pink with lots of big yellow and purple flowers.

He'll look so *pretty* in it, she thought.

She brought it to her room and laid it delicately on her bed. She dragged her desk chair to her closet, stood on it, and got her camera down from the shelf.

It was the type of camera that developed the pictures itself in sixty seconds. She checked to make sure it was loaded.

Her eyes turned to the muumuu. "Just divine," she said out loud. It was large enough that Gabriel could wear it over his clothes. He would just have to roll up his pant legs and shirt sleeves so they wouldn't show, and take off his shoes and socks.

She wondered why the dress was called a muumuu. Maybe because it's big enough for a cow! she thought. Moo moo. She smiled at her joke. She'd have to remember to tell it to Gabriel.

She made sure her parents weren't watching, then brought the camera and the dress out back to the Dog House. She draped the dress over the television and put the camera on top of it. She returned to her room and waited.

Gabriel stood outside the front door. *Maybe*, he hoped. What if Laura found out he really didn't know anything about Pig City? He wondered what she meant by insurance. Somehow, he had to get her to explain it all to him, then act like he already knew it. Maybe, maybe, maybe, maybe, maybe . . . . Laura, Laura, Laura, Laura, Laura. He rang the doorbell.

"I got it!" Laura shouted. She ran down the hall, past her mother. She stopped just before the door. She took off her cap, wiped her hair back off her face, then put the cap back on. She opened the door.

"Hi," said Gabriel.

She was glad Gabriel knew all about Pig City. She wouldn't have to go through a lot of explanations. "C'mon, let's go to the Dog House."

"To the Dog House," said Gabriel.

They went through the living room, which was a big mistake. Her parents stopped them and asked her to introduce him to them, and then everybody said how nice it was to meet each other. Laura waited impatiently.

They went out the back door. "Yep, there's the Dog House," said Gabriel. There was no mistaking it. He walked inside. She followed.

He sat in the swinging chair.

She was going to tell him that that was her chair, but then she decided it didn't matter. She sat on the bed. She glanced quickly at the dress and camera lying on the television, then her eyes turned to Gabriel.

He swiveled around in the chair, looking at everything.

"What do you think?" she asked him.

"Just as I expected," he said.

"Okay, here's the thing," said Laura. "Even though you already know about Pig City, you still have to give insurance, just to make it official."

"Right. I know that," he said.

Laura smiled. She got the treasure chest out from under the bed. "You know what this is?" she asked.

"A treasure chest," said Gabriel.

Laura nodded. "Inside are the Treasures of Pig City," she said. "It's where we put everybody's insurance." She sat back down on the bed.

Gabriel snapped his fingers. "Oh, I just remembered," he said. "I left my insurance at home. Why don't you let me use somebody else's insurance for now, and then I'll bring my own insurance to school tomorrow."

"What are you talking about?"

"Nothing. Never mind."

"I pick your insurance," said Laura. "You don't get to bring your own."

"Right. I knew that," said Gabriel. "I was making a joke."

"Okay," said Laura. She looked at the muumuu. She wondered if Gabriel would really agree to wear it. She thought about Aaron and Nathan, how quickly they had agreed to do what they were told. But Gabriel was different. Aaron and Nathan were followers. Gabriel was a leader.

"Okay, here's the thing," said Laura. "Now you have to agree to do whatever I say."

"I will."

"Once I tell you what your insurance is, you can't change your mind."

"I won't."

"Okay, here's the thing," said Laura. She stopped.

"What?" he asked.

"Okay, this is what you have to do."

"What?"

She took off her cap and wiped her hair off her face. The hat stayed off.

"What do I have to do?" he asked.

"You have to kiss me."

# PART TWO

# The Monkey Town Wars

# 20
# The Kiss

*They remained* where they 'were, Gabriel in the swinging chair, Laura on the bed.

Gabriel said, "What?"

"You heard me," Laura whispered.

It had surprised her almost as much as it had Gabriel, and she was the one who said it. She was all set to tell him he had to put on the muumuu, but somehow those other words came out.

They stayed glued to their chairs.

The best way to explain Laura's change of heart is like this: Before, she had to kiss him. Now, he had to kiss her. That was a big difference.

She took a deep breath. She felt her heart beating. She imagined herself kissing him, then raising her fist to her nose and saying very sexily, "Welcome to Pig City."

"What's so funny?" Gabriel asked.

She shook her head. She hadn't realized she was smiling.

They stared into each other's eyes.

Gabriel climbed out of the swinging chair.

Laura stood up. She felt tingly all over. "Have you ever kissed a girl before?" she whispered.

"No," he said. "Have you?"

She laughed.

He did, too. "I mean, have you ever kissed a boy?"

She shook her head. "I never would have chosen it for your insurance," she said, "except it was your idea in the first place."

"What do you mean?"

"You know. What you said in the note you wrote me."

"What are you talking about?" Gabriel's voice was an octave higher than usual. He cleared his throat.

"You know," said Laura.

"No, I don't." His voice was still way up there.

"You said if I didn't kiss you, you'd tell everyone about Pig City." Thinking about it again made her angry.

"What are you talking about?"

Laura put her hands on her hips and stared at him. She recited the note from memory. " 'Hey Laura, I know all about Pig City. If you don't kiss me, I will tell the whole school. You have ugly hair. Your humble servant, Gabriel.' "

"Are you crazy?" Gabriel asked.

"You wrote it, not me," said Laura.

"I never said you had to *kiss* me!"

"Don't lie to *me*," said Laura. "*I* read it, remember. You put it in *my* desk."

"You're the one who's lying," said Gabriel.

That did it. Nobody called her a liar. "Get out!" she exclaimed. "You're not allowed in Pig City! I'll never kiss you! And you're too ugly to wear a dress!"

"Yeah, well you're too ugly to wear a suit and tie!" snapped Gabriel.

They shouted at each other, using every bad word they knew and some they didn't know.

"If you cut your hair every time you told a lie, you'd be bald!" said Gabriel.

"Get out!" Laura screamed. "Liars aren't allowed in the Dog House!"

"Then what are you still doing here?"

"You're repulsive," she said. "No girl will ever want to kiss you, not for your whole life."

"At least I didn't kiss you. I probably would have gotten warts all over my face."

"You are a wart."

"You're a canker sore."

"Get out of here! Go crawl back where you came from."

"Oink, oink," said Gabriel.

"That's so stupid."

"Oink, oink," he repeated. He stepped out and slammed the door behind him. It bounced back open.

Laura remained alone in the Dog House. She tore her sister's purple and pink Hawaiian muumuu to shreds.

# 21
# Slow Torture

*Laura stared* through the hole in her cinnamon doughnut. It had been three days since her fight with Gabriel. She'd hardly slept or eaten anything since. She felt like she was losing control.

As far as she knew, Gabriel hadn't told anybody about Pig City, *yet*. She knew he would. Still, she continued to write her messages on the board. On Tuesday she wrote, PIGS FOREVER! and on Wednesday, PIGS ARE WINNERS! She had to. If she didn't, the citizens of Pig City would know something was wrong. And she couldn't let Gabriel know she was afraid of him. But the more messages she put up, the more dictionary pages she'd have to copy when he finally told.

He kept almost telling. He'd raise his hand as if he was going to tell on her, but instead he'd make some kind of ordinary comment. She knew he was doing it on purpose, to torture her.

"Don't you think you should eat something a little more substantial for breakfast than just a doughnut?" asked her mother.

"Let me make you an egg," offered her father.

"No!" she screamed.

"Laura!" scolded her mother.

"I'm sorry," she said quietly. "You know I hate eggs." She was almost in tears.

All her life, it seemed, people were trying to force eggs down her throat. "I know you don't like it soft-boiled, but try it hard-boiled," they'd say. Or, "Try my egg salad, it doesn't taste like eggs." Or, "Have you ever tasted quiche? It's nothing like regular eggs." No matter how you cook it, an egg is an egg is an egg.

She sighed. She knew it wasn't eggs that had her so upset. It was Gabriel, the biggest rotten egg of them all.

"Oh, I know what's the matter with Laura," said her father.

"Nothing's the matter!" she snapped.

"Remember that boy who came by the other evening?" her father continued. "What was his name? Gabriel?"

She stared at him in horror.

"So?" said her mother.

"It's obvious," said her father. "She doesn't eat. She doesn't sleep." He smiled. "Laura's in love."

She screamed.

She went to school and sneaked into Mr. Doyle's room. The number 6 was next to the rectangle under the word DICTIONARY. Her hand shook as she wrote PIGS ARE SUPREME in the center of the black-board. There was no way she could copy six — make that seven, dictionary pages.

Everyone laughed when they saw her message. "It sounds like something you'd eat at Jack in the Box," laughed Karen. "A Pig Supreme!"

Mr. Doyle erased it and told the class to settle down. He put the number 7 next to the rectangle. "Yes, Gabriel."

Gabriel lowered his hand. "I have something to say about those things that somebody keeps writing on the board," he said.

Laura closed her eyes.

"I don't think they're very funny," Gabriel said. "Everybody always laughs, but I don't think we should. It disrupts the class and just encourages whoever is writing them. Like today's, 'Pigs Are Supreme.' What's funny about that? Nothing."

"Thank you, Gabriel," said Mr. Doyle. "Your point is well taken."

Gabriel turned and smiled at Laura. He brought his fist to his nose and lowered it.

She pretended not to notice. Her leg was shaking. She almost wished Gabriel would tell Mr. Doyle and get it over with.

Just before recess, he raised his hand again.

"Yes, Gabriel."

"Oh, I was just stretching," he said. "I wasn't raising my hand."

Laura walked very slowly out to recess. She stood on the steps in front of the school and watched the other members of Pig City salute each other; five girls and two boys. She was their leader. Somehow, she had to be strong. George Washington never complained about the cold weather when he was at Valley Forge.

"Laura?" someone said behind her.

She turned to see Karen.

"Would it be okay if I joined Pig City?" Karen asked.

Laura stared at her, thunderstruck.

"Yolanda said I should ask you," said Karen. "She said you're the president."

Laura called Allison and Tiffany over and asked Karen to repeat what she had said to them.

"I asked Laura if I could join Pig City," said Karen.

They were aghast.

"And why did you ask me?" asked Laura.

"Yolanda said you're the president," said Karen. "She told me to ask you. What's the matter? Did I say something wrong?"

For the first time in three days, Laura smiled.

# 22
# Dancing on the Edge
# of a Razor Blade

*Dearest Darling Jonathan,*
*    I'm madly in love with you. I dream about*
*kissing you all the time. You're so handsome.*
*I'd love to run my fingers through your hair.*
                        *Love,*
                        *Yolanda*


Laura placed the note inside Jonathan's desk.

Yolanda was so shy, Laura couldn't imagine what she'd do. Maybe she'll run away and become a nun, she thought.

But Yolanda knew the rules. She knew this would happen if she told anybody about Pig City, even Karen.

It might have been the worst thing that could

have happened to Yolanda, but it was the best thing that could have happened to Laura. Now, if Gabriel blabbed about Pig City, Yolanda would be blamed for it, or Karen. Laura would still have to copy seven dictionary pages, but that was the least of her worries. Seven dictionary pages no longer seemed like a lot to her. Make that eight!

She went to the blackboard and tried to think of something great to write. Nothing came to her.

Laura stared foolishly at the blackboard. She began to get nervous. It was silly, but she couldn't think of anything to write. Her mind was blank.

It was getting late. She had to write something and get out of there quickly. Think, Laura, think, she thought.

She wrote something, then shoved the piece of chalk into her pants pocket and hurried out of the room. She walked a little too quickly. Several teachers looked at her suspiciously, but didn't say anything.

Allison and Tiffany were outside waiting for her. "Did you put it in his desk?" asked Allison.

Laura took off her cap, wiped her hair back off her face, then put the cap back on. "Yes."

Tiffany shrieked.

The other members of Pig City were standing around the tetherball pole. There was no tetherball, only a pole.

Everyone raised and lowered their fists.

"Laura has an important announcement to make," Tiffany announced.

Everyone waited.

"I'm afraid I have some bad news," said Laura.

Tiffany and Allison smiled.

Laura looked at Yolanda, standing quietly with her hands folded in front of her. "Yolanda is no longer a member of Pig City," Laura stated. "She has violated our sacred trust! She has broken her vow of secrecy!"

Everyone looked at Yolanda.

"What?" she uttered. "I didn't. . . ."

"You told Karen!" Tiffany accused.

Yolanda's golden skin turned white. She looked from one person to another. "But she — I mean, Karen wouldn't — "

"We have already redeemed your insurance," said Laura.

Yolanda put her hands over her face, then ran away.

"What was Yolanda's insurance?" asked Kristin.

"She had to write a love letter to a boy," said Allison.

Tiffany giggled.

"Which boy?" asked Nathan.

"Jonathan," Debbie asserted.

Laura looked at Debbie. "How did you know?"

"Was I right?" asked Debbie. "I knew it! Yolanda's been in love with Jonathan since the fourth grade. Except she's so shy."

"What'd the letter say?" asked Kristin.

Laura was too embarrassed to repeat it in front of the boys.

Tiffany wasn't. " 'Dearest Darling Jonathan,' " She giggled. " 'I'm madly in love with you!' " She laughed harder. " 'I dream about kissing you all the time!' " She was hysterical. " 'You're so handsome!' " She fell to her knees, unable to finish.

Everyone else was laughing with her.

Tiffany covered her face with her hands and squealed, " 'I'd love to run my fingers through your hair!' "

Kristin and Nathan screamed.

"Where's the note?" asked Aaron.

"I put it in Jonathan's desk," said Laura.

"Oh, no!" exclaimed Kristin.

Everyone hooted and howled. Nathan lay on the ground and pounded the blacktop with his fist. Kristin hugged the tetherball pole.

No one noticed Mr. Doyle, who walked up to them and stood with his arms crossed, watching. "Glad to see you're all so happy," he said at last.

They stopped laughing. "Good morning, Mr. Doyle," said Nathan.

"Good morning, Nathan, Tiffany, Allison, Debbie, *Laura*. I wonder. Do you think there's anything written on the board this morning, Laura?"

"Yes, I do," she replied.

"And what is that?" he asked.

"There's the word 'Dictionary,' " she said, "and under that is a rectangle and next to that is the number seven."

"Yes, that's still there, isn't it? But one of these days there will be a name in the rectangle. A word to the wise." He smiled and headed back toward the school building.

"He knows!" whispered Debbie. "He knows it's you."

"He only thinks he knows," said Nathan. "He doesn't know he knows."

Laura smiled confidently. She stuck her hand in her pocket and felt the piece of chalk. The smile dropped off her face.

She didn't remember sticking the chalk in her pocket. That was a stupid thing to do. She had made a mistake. If Mr. Doyle had seen it, then he would have had all the proof he needed.

"What's wrong, Laura?" asked Allison.

She shook her head.

They lined up for class. Yolanda was ahead of them in line, next to Karen. Gabriel was behind them.

Laura was dancing on the edge of a razor blade. She couldn't afford to make mistakes.

She heard the kids ahead of her laugh when they entered the room. She smiled. She was glad they liked her message, especially after Gabriel's speech.

She pushed through the yellow curtain and glanced at the board. Then she looked at it again. Then she looked at it a third time. Written in the center of the board were the words:

PIGS STINK!

The citizens of Pig City were all staring at her. They wore big questions marks on their faces.

# 23
# Poor Yolanda

*Laura was stunned.* She put her hand down on somebody's desk to steady herself.

"Get your fat paw off my desk!" said Sheila.

Laura regained control. She let her hand rest on Sheila's desk for a second longer than necessary, then elegantly raised it, like a queen might raise her hand for a knight to kiss. Her long hair swished in Sheila's face as she turned and walked to her seat.

I know I didn't write that, she thought. I wrote PIGS THINK, didn't I? She wasn't sure. She remembered how flustered she became when she couldn't think of anything to write. She stuck the chalk in her pocket without realizing it. Is it possible I wrote PIGS STINK instead of PIGS THINK?

She closed her eyes and tried to get a picture of

the blackboard, the way it was earlier, in her mind. Nothing came to her.

Okay, if I didn't write it, who else could have written it? The answer came to her instantly. She turned and looked at Gabriel.

He was looking straight ahead. His face gave away nothing.

Well, if he wrote it, that's good. Then he can't tell on *me* for writing on the board anymore.

Her eyes went from Gabriel to Sheila sitting behind him. She could have written it, too, Laura realized. Sheila hates me. But she doesn't know about Pig City. Unless Gabriel told her.

In front of Gabriel sat Karen. Karen knew about Pig City. Maybe Karen wrote it because we wouldn't let her join. Or Yolanda because we gave her note to Jonathan.

She wondered if Jonathan had found the note yet. She could see only the back of Jonathan's blond head. His ears looked a little red.

PIGS STINK remained on the board. Mr. Doyle had changed the number next to the rectangle from 7 to 8 but didn't erase the message.

Aha! she thought triumphantly. You think you're so clever, don't you! Well, it won't work, Mr. Doyle! You don't fool me.

It had to be Mr. Doyle who wrote it, she realized. It was a trick to try and trap her. That was why he hadn't erased it.

Good try, Mr. Doyle! Laura thought. She had it all figured out. He would leave the message up there all day, staring at her, trying to break her. He wanted her to admit she wrote the other messages by saying that someone had changed what she had

written. You must think I'm really stupid, Mr. Doyle.
He erased the board.

Laura shook her head. I must be going crazy.


"Why'd you write 'Pigs Stink'?" Allison asked, fist on nose, on their way out to recess.

"I didn't write it." She hoped it wasn't a lie. If she said something she thought was true, but realized it might have been false, and then it turned out to be false, did that make it a lie? She shook her head. Now I'm thinking like Nathan! I don't even make sense to myself.

Debbie approached. Fists went to noses and back again.

"Why'd you write 'Pigs Stink'?" asked Debbie.

"She didn't write it," said Allison.

"I wrote 'Pigs Think,' " said Laura. "Somebody changed it."

"Who?" asked Debbie.

She shrugged.

"Hey, why'd you write 'Pigs Stink'?" demanded Tiffany.

Laura waited for everyone to gather, then told them all for the last time that she didn't write it, and she didn't know who did.

"It has to be someone who knows about Pig City," said Kristin.

"Yolanda!" declared Debbie. "Because of what we did to her."

"Maybe," said Laura. "But she didn't find out until just before class started. I don't know if she had time."

"How about Karen?" said Tiffany. "She knows about us, too. And we wouldn't let her join."

"Yolanda or Karen could have told somebody else," said Aaron. "It could be anybody."

"It doesn't have to be somebody who knows anything about us," said Nathan. "I mean, Laura's been writing stuff about pigs every day. Maybe it's just someone who's sick of seeing how great pigs are. I mean — "

"Spit it out," said Debbie.

"Whatever happened with Gabriel?" asked Tiffany.

"Mr. Doyle might have written it," said Laura.

"Mr. Doyle?" they all said together.

"Yes, Mr. Doyle," Laura answered. "He's trying to trick me into admitting that I'm the one who's been writing all the pig messages, by making me deny that I wrote 'Pigs Stink.' "

"That makes sense," said Nathan.

"Not to me it doesn't," said Kristin.

"I want to know what Gabriel knows," said Tiffany.

"Why Gabriel?" asked Aaron.

"Laura was going to ask him to join," Tiffany explained. "Each of us was supposed to ask a boy. I asked Nathan, Allison asked you, and Laura was supposed to ask Gabriel."

"I told you," said Laura. "I changed my mind."

"But you never said why," said Tiffany.

"Yes, she did," said Allison. "She said she hated him."

"But she said that before, too," Tiffany pointed out.

"It could have been Gabriel," Laura admitted. "It could have been like Nathan said. Gabriel got tired of seeing all the pig messages, so he changed

'Pigs Think' to 'Pigs Stink' because he thought it was funny."

"That's right!" exclaimed Nathan. "That's what I said. Or at least what I meant to say."

"Well in that case, it could be anybody," said Tiffany.

"It could even have been one of us," Nathan whispered.

They looked at each other suspiciously.

Laura wondered about Debbie. There was something about Debbie that bothered her. She remembered how Debbie knew Yolanda's note was written to Jonathan before anyone told her.

"Look!" exclaimed Kristin.

Everyone turned.

Yolanda and Jonathan were walking across the playground together, *holding hands*.

# 24
# A Turkey Playing Football

*"Nathan's so cute,"* said Tiffany. "Every time he sees me, he touches his nose with his fist."

"So, we all do that," said Allison.

"But Nathan's so cuuute!" said Tiffany.

Laura and Allison laughed. They were walking home from school. The Mystery of the Altered Message was never solved.

"Do you think Yolanda did it on purpose?" Laura asked.

"What do you mean?" asked Allison.

"Remember Debbie said that Yolanda's been in love with Jonathan since the fourth grade. Then yesterday, Karen said Yolanda *told* her to ask me if she could join Pig City. Yolanda knew what would happen."

"She knew you'd put her note in Jonathan's

desk," said Allison. "She wanted you to do it!" She covered her mouth with her hand, then took it away. "Remember how quickly she chose Jonathan?"

"She might have done it all on purpose," said Laura, "without even realizing she was doing it."

"Ooh, I just got a chill down my back," said Tiffany. "It's like she has a split personality. Part of her is very shy and scared of boys, but she has a burning desire buried deep beneath her breasts!" She covered her heart with her hands.

"Yolanda doesn't have a split personality," said Allison.

"She doesn't even have breasts," said Laura.

They all laughed.

"Do you think boys really care about that?" Tiffany asked. "I mean do you think a boy wouldn't like a girl if she was flat?"

Allison shrugged. "I don't know what's so special about boobs! Anyway, none of the girls in our class have very much."

"Except Sheila," said Tiffany. "Maybe that's why Gabriel likes her. 'Cause she's stacked!"

"Does Gabriel like Sheila?" asked Laura. She tried not to sound too interested.

"Oh, I don't know," said Tiffany. "I saw them talking after school."

They reached the corner where Tiffany and Allison went one way and Laura the other. Fists met noses, then Laura walked the rest of the way home alone. It was Friday, but she couldn't hang out with her friends because company was coming over.

She had an uneasy feeling in the pit of her stomach. She knew it was because of Gabriel and Sheila.

She tried to ignore it. It was stupid. She had no reason to be jealous. She took off her cap, shook her hair back, and put the cap back on.

The feeling remained.

"Aunt Laura!" Rebecca greeted her, as she entered the house.

Laura smiled. She loved it when Rebecca called her that.

Rebecca was five years old. She was the daughter of Laura's oldest brother, Dan, and his wife, Sue. They were all spending the weekend.

"What's Pig City?" Sue asked.

"I got it at a garage sale," said Laura, not about to break her vow of secrecy.

"She never takes it off," said her mother.

"I don't think she really likes it," said her father. "I think it's stuck to her head, and she's afraid to tell anyone."

Laura laughed even though she didn't think it was funny.

The feeling remained inside her. It stayed with her all weekend, gnawing at the insides of her stomach.

On Sunday, she received two earth-shattering phone calls. The first one was good news. It made her sad. The second was bad news. It made her glad.

Tiffany called first. "Laura!" she exclaimed. "You'll never guess what happened! Nathan came over to see me today. Actually he came over to see Hubert."

"Your hamster?" questioned Laura. She lay with her head at the foot of the bed. Her feet were on her pillow.

"Uh-huh," said Tiffany. "Nathan likes hamsters. He likes all animals. His favorite is the porcupine. See, first he called and asked about the homework assignment."

"We never have homework over the weekend," said Laura.

"He forgot what day it was," Tiffany explained. "He thought it was Tuesday. Did you know that Saturday is his favorite day of the week, and it's mine, too? Isn't that a coinc-i-dinc? That's what Nathan says instead of 'coincidence.' I like Sunday second, but he likes Friday. Do you want to hear his order for the rest of the days?"

"That's okay."

"We told each other our favorite colors and our favorite food and our favorite animals, and that's when I told him I had a hamster named Hubert. He said he liked hamsters, and I asked him if he wanted to meet Hubert, and he said, 'Okee-dokee-do.' So he came over to meet Hubert. They liked each other."

"Nathan and Hubert?"

"Hamsters can tell about people," said Tiffany. "They know if someone's nice or not. So anyway, now I'm getting to the good part. After Nathan finished talking to Hubert, we went out in the backyard, and we were just kind of lying on the grass talking and looking up at the sky. We kept picking out things we saw in the clouds, you know, like giraffes and camels and a whale with a spout, and a lamp on top of the spout, and a turkey playing football."

"A what?"

Tiffany laughed. "A turkey playing football! I

didn't see it at first, but Nathan showed it to me, and then once I saw it, it looked just like a turkey playing football! Really!"

"What does a turkey playing football look like?"

"I don't know, like a turkey playing football. Wait, I'm getting to the good part now. Anyway, so then I saw a fish driving a car. He said he didn't see it, so I showed it to him again, but he said, 'I still don't see it,' and I said, 'See, the fish's hands are on the steering wheel,' and he said, 'No, show me,' and I had to put my head right next to his so he could see where I was pointing, and then just as I was trying to show him, Laura, he kissed me!"

Laura gasped.

Tiffany squealed.

"On the lips?" asked Laura.

"Yep. It happened so fast. One second I was pointing to the sky and the next, smack! You know, I bet he saw the fish the whole time."

Laura laughed. "Probably," she said.

"So then, we just stared up at the clouds some more without saying anything. Then he went home. We both said, 'See you tomorrow,' at the exact same time! It was funny."

"Kissing him?" asked Laura.

"No! Saying, 'See you tomorrow,' at the same time."

Laura didn't think it was funny.

"I'm a different person now than I was yester-day," Tiffany said very seriously.

"What do you mean?"

"It's hard to explain. You wouldn't understand. Well, I've got to call Allison and tell her. 'Bye!"

" 'Bye."

Laura hung up. She felt terrible. She knew she should feel happy for her friend, but she didn't, and that made her feel even more rotten. "You wouldn't understand," Tiffany had said.

She walked to the bathroom and looked at herself in the mirror. It didn't seem fair. She was prettier than Tiffany or Allison. She should have been the first to kiss a boy.

"Fish don't have hands!" she said aloud.

Everybody had a boyfriend except for her. Tiffany and Nathan. Allison and Aaron. Yolanda and Jonathan. "Sheila's as ugly as a toad!"

"Who's Sheila?" asked Rebecca.

Laura turned around, startled. "Nobody," she muttered.

She wondered if she'd ever kiss a boy. What if next year in junior high no boy would want to kiss her because she didn't have experience?

She went into her parents' bedroom, where she found her father reading a book. "Do you think I'm pretty?" she asked.

He said yes. She asked him, "How pretty?" and he told her she was the most beautiful girl in the world. She asked if he was just saying that because she was his daughter, and he said he wasn't. They went on that way for over fifteen minutes, until she was practically talking baby talk. It was sickening.

Worst of all, Laura knew it was sickening. She heard herself talking to her father, and she hated herself for it. Still she continued.

When she left her father, she found her mother and had almost the identical conversation with her. Fortunately, her phone rang again.

It's probably Allison telling me Aaron kissed her! she thought bitterly as she walked to her room.

"Hello."

There was no one there. "Hello," she repeated. "Hello."

Nothing. She hung up.

She sighed. She felt like she was about to cry.

The phone rang again. "Hello!" she demanded.

"Monkey Town will turn Pig City into bacon and eggs," said a voice. There was some muffled laughter, then the line went dead.

She slowly hung up the phone. *Monkey Town will turn Pig City into bacon and eggs.* She hadn't recognized the voice. It was disguised to sound like a cranky old lady.

Later when she came to dinner, everybody made a point of telling her how pretty she looked.

"You're going to break a lot of hearts someday," said her brother Dan.

"You get prettier every time I see you," said Sue.

Even Rebecca got in the act. "You're the prettiest of all my aunts and uncles," she said. "You're much prettier than Sheila!"

"Knock it off, okay?" said Laura. She didn't care whether or not she was pretty!

George Washington didn't worry about whether or not a girl would ever want to kiss him. That was probably a good thing, too, Laura thought. What girl would want to kiss somebody with wooden teeth?

The fire returned to her eyes. Pig City was going to war!

106

# 25
# Monkey Town

*"Bacon and eggs?"* asked Gabriel.

Karen laughed.

"Sorry, Gabe," said Howard.

"Pigs don't lay eggs, Howard," said Jonathan.

Howard was supposed to have called Laura and said, "Monkey Town will turn Pig City into bacon and ham." That made sense. Bacon and ham come from slaughtered pigs.

Howard felt awful. He was so happy when Gabriel asked him to join the club, but now he messed up his first assignment. "I meant to say ham," he explained. "It's more natural to say 'bacon and eggs' than 'bacon and ham.' It's hard to say 'bacon and ham.' "

"Bacon and ham. Bacon and ham. Bacon and ham," said Sheila.

107

"You want me to call her back, Gabe?" asked Howard. "I can call her back and tell her I meant ham."

Karen laughed hysterically.

"This is war, Howard," said Gabriel. "We can't call her back and say we made a mistake."

"It might be better this way," said Jonathan. "They're not just pigs. They're chicken pigs! They lay eggs."

Everyone laughed.

"They still won't know what 'bacon and eggs' means," said Yolanda.

"That's all right," said Gabriel. "One of the first rules of war is to confuse the enemy. You did a good job, Howard."

"I knew you'd like it," said Howard. "That's why I did it."

Sheila snorted.

"We'll have to change our song," said Yolanda. "What rhymes with eggs?"

"Pegs," said Jonathan.

"Begs," said Karen.

"I think we should just tell Mr. Doyle that Laura's the one who wrote on the board," said Sheila.

"We can't," said Gabriel. "I wrote on the board, too. I wrote 'Pigs Stink.' If she gets in trouble, we all will." He would never have told on Laura, anyway, but he had to give a reason that would satisfy Sheila.

"There's more than one way to skin a pig," he said. He stuck his right thumb in his right ear and wiggled the remaining fingers on that hand.

Everyone else did the same.

It was the secret Monkey Town salute.

# 26
# Eye of the Hurricane

*Laura walked* to school Monday morning, alert, but not afraid. She didn't know who or what Monkey Town was, or what bacon and eggs meant. She was ready for anything.

She sneaked into the building and on through the yellow curtain into Mr. Doyle's room. There was already a message on the board:

MONKEYS ARE
MARVELOUS
MAGNIFICENT
AND MIRACULOUS!

She picked up the eraser and a piece of chalk. She didn't change it all, just enough.

She placed the eraser and chalk back on the rack, then walked calmly out through the school to the outside. She stood with her back against the brick wall so nobody could sneak up behind her, and waited for Pig City. Her eyes moved constantly.

Tiffany and Allison came walking across the blacktop. She went out to meet them and raised her fist to her nose.

Allison returned the salute. Tiffany didn't. Something was wrong. Tiffany looked very scared and confused.

Laura wondered if Monkey Town had gotten to her already. "Are you all right?" she asked.

"I don't know what to say to him!" Tiffany complained, pulling at her hair. "How can I even look at him?"

"Look at who?" asked Laura.

"Nathan!" Tiffany exclaimed. "Who else?"

Laura laughed.

Allison shrugged. "She started out perfectly normal, or at least, normal for Tiffany. Then the closer we got to school, the crazier she got. She's afraid to see Nathan, after you know, what they did."

"It's not funny!" Tiffany insisted. "Tell me what to say to him, Laura."

"I don't know," Laura replied. "*I wouldn't understand*, remember?"

"Just talk to him like you always did," said Allison. "Say what you used to say."

"I can't remember what I used to say," complained Tiffany.

Debbie and Kristin approached. Everyone saluted. Tiffany missed. Her fist hit her eye.

"Did anybody else get a call from Monkey Town?" Laura asked.

"Monkey Town?" questioned Debbie.

Laura told them about the phone call.

"Bacon and eggs?" asked Kristin. "What does that mean?"

"I don't know," said Laura. "But it doesn't sound good."

Tiffany gasped.

Everyone turned around.

It was Nathan. He and Aaron were approaching. Nathan's face was as red as a beet.

They all saluted. Tiffany punched herself in the nose.

"Hi, Tiffany," said Nathan.

"Hi, Nathan," said Tiffany.

"Hi," said Nathan. "How's your hamster?"

"Fine, thank you," said Tiffany, "and yours?"

"Fine, thank you," said Nathan, even though he didn't own a hamster.

Laura repeated her news about Monkey Town for Nathan's and Aaron's benefit. "We all have to be very careful," she warned.

As they lined up for class, Tiffany pulled Laura aside. "That wasn't so bad, was it?" she said. "We talked just like always."

"I guess you're both too busy worrying about Monkey Town to worry about each other," said Laura.

"Monkey Town?" asked Tiffany. "What's that?"

They went inside. Nobody laughed at the message on the blackboard. Nobody knew what it meant.

MONKEY ARE
MARVELOUS
MAGNIFICENT
AND MUSTARD!

"Mustard!" exclaimed Karen.

"Is something bothering you, Karen?" asked Mr. Doyle.

"Uh, no, Mr. Doyle. Um, I don't like mustard."

"Do you like ketchup?" he asked.

"It's okay."

"Good, I'm glad you have something to put on your hot dog." He erased the board and put the number 9 next to the rectangle under the word DICTIONARY.

"There's an egg in my desk!" Kristin announced.

Several kids laughed.

"Kristin?" said Mr. Doyle.

She showed him the egg.

Laura found an egg in her desk, too. It was hard-boiled, without the shell.

"Hey, I got one, too," said Aaron. He held up his egg.

"Does anybody else have an egg?" asked Mr. Doyle.

Everybody looked inside his or her desk. Five people raised their hands and eggs: Debbie, Nathan, Tiffany, Allison, and Laura. The entire population of Pig City had been *egg-laid*.

They brought their eggs to Mr. Doyle. He asked them how the eggs got in their desks, but they all said they didn't know. They returned to their seats.

"All right," said Mr. Doyle. "We've had enough silliness for one morning. Now, I want to know where these eggs came from!"

Gabriel raised his hand.

"Gabriel," said Mr. Doyle.

"Chickens," said Gabriel.

For a moment, Mr. Doyle looked like he was going to explode, then he smiled. "That's very good, Gabriel," he admitted. "I set myself up for that one."

He addressed the class. "This happens every year just about this time," he said.

"People find eggs in their desks?" asked Linzy.

"No," said Mr. Doyle. "Sixth-graders go crazy. We have only three weeks until graduation, so everybody starts thinking that they're pretty hot stuff. You think you can do anything. Well, let me give you a word to the wise. Your grades count more now than they did at the beginning of the year. If you fail your tests, you may be left back. If you break the rules, you will be punished. Anyone who owes me a dictionary page at the end of the year will not graduate. If you think I'm bluffing, go talk to some of my former students." He looked out across the room. "A word to the wise."

Laura smiled. Who are you trying to kid? she thought.

At recess, Pig City discussed how to best strike back at Monkey Town.

"We don't even know who they are," said Kristin.

"But they know who we are," said Aaron. "The eggs proved that."

"There might be hundreds of them," said Nathan.

"Why eggs?" asked Debbie. "What do eggs mean?"

Nobody knew.

"What does mustard mean?" asked Aaron.

"I wrote that," said Laura. "It means they're yellow! They're chicken!"

"Do you think they'll be able to figure that out?" asked Debbie.

"That doesn't matter," said Laura. "It's better if they can't. They'll worry more."

Suddenly everyone stopped talking. Gabriel, Sheila, Karen, Jonathan, Yolanda, and Howard were coming toward them.

"One, two, three . . ." said Gabriel.

They snapped their fingers and sang:

*"Monkey town! (snap-snap)*
*Monkey town! (snap-snap)*
*We're the greatest club around! (snap-snap)*

*Monkey town! (snap-snap)*
*Monkey town! (snap-snap)*
*Gonna turn Pig City upside-down! (snap-snap)*

Pigs *walk on (snap-snap)*
four *legs! (snap-snap)*
*They're nothing but*
*BACON and EGGS! (snap-snap)*

*Monkey town! (snap-snap)*
*Monkey town! (snap-snap)*
*We're the greatest club around! (snap-snap)"*

"You mustard!" shouted Nathan.

They sang louder and changed from snapping fingers to clapping their hands.

*''Monkey town! (clap-clap)*
*Monkey town! (clap-clap)*
*Gonna turn Pig City UPSIDE-DOWN! (clap-clap)*
*Pigs walk on (clap-clap) four legs! (clap-clap)''*

"Monkeys are mustard!" screamed Debbie. Everyone in Pig City began shouting it. "Monkeys are mustard! Monkeys are mustard!"

"THEY'RE NOTHING BUT BACON AND EGGS!!!" sang Monkey Town as loud as they could scream.

Good, now we know who they are, thought Laura, calm amidst the chaos. She was the eye of the hurricane.

# 27
# War!

*The war raged* all week. By Friday, every pencil belonging to the citizens of Monkey Town and Pig City had been broken.

It started Monday after recess, when Howard accidentally dropped his pencil. It rolled under his chair and behind him. Debbie reached down and grabbed it, then broke it in half.

After that, no pencil was safe. If anybody left his or her pencil unguarded, for even a second, it would be snatched and snapped.

Besides pencil-breaking, there was a lot of name-calling, some apple-core-throwing, one home-work-stealing, many attempted cap-liftings, and a day of mud-splashing.

It was Tiffany's homework that was stolen. Jonathan and Yolanda changed all the answers, then returned it to her without her knowing it. She didn't find out until Mr. Doyle returned it to her with a big red zero on top.

The mud-splashing occurred on Wednesday after it had rained heavily on Tuesday night. Jonathan was shooting baskets before school. He tossed the basketball high in the air. It was a perfect shot. The ball landed in the center of a mud puddle, just as Aaron passed by. Mud splattered all over his clean clothes.

As Jonathan and Yolanda were laughing, Debbie picked up Jonathan's books, which he had left at the edge of the court, and threw them in the mud.

Gabriel ran up behind her and stamped his foot into the mud, getting himself muddy, but Debbie muddier.

It continued all day. Only Laura's cap remained mud-free. It never left her head, despite numerous attempts by Monkey Town to steal it. Her cap became the most prized possession of the war. It was Pig City's flag. As long as she wore it, Pig City was the land of the free and the home of the brave.

Thursday, Allison opened her lunch sack and saw a pin sticking through the side of her carton of fruit punch, near the bottom. To everyone's amazement, none of the punch had leaked out. "Do you think it's safe to drink?" she asked.

"Take the pin out first," cautioned Tiffany.

Allison removed the pin, and the punch leaked out the hole and onto her lap.

All week, Monkey Town continued to sing their song over and over and over again. Laura hated that more than anything else.

It was like a stupid song you hear on the radio

or a silly jingle from a television commercial. No matter how much you hate it, you catch yourself humming it all the time.

It drove her crazy. When she went to bed at night, she'd hear her brain singing, *"Monkey Town. Monkey Town. Gonna turn Pig City upside-down."*

We'll see who turns who upside-down! she thought angrily.

The morning messages didn't stop.

Tuesday: MONKEYS ARE MORONS
Wednesday: PIGS PICK THEIR NOSES
Thursday: MONKEYS CHEW THEIR TAILS
Friday: PIGS WEAR WIGS

Those were the messages that everyone got to see, anyway. Each message had been changed at least once, usually twice or three times, as Gabriel and Laura sneaked back and forth into the room one after the other in a dangerous game of chicken. On Friday, the last change was made from PIGS ARE WISE to PIGS WEAR WIGS only seconds before the bell rang.

The number 13 was placed next to the rectangle under DICTIONARY.

After lunch on Friday, Laura led Pig City around the side of the school to the door through which she entered every morning. "Now, nobody act suspicious," she cautioned. "Pretend you're supposed to be here." They sneaked inside.

The school was much more crowded during lunch than it was early in the morning. Teachers were everywhere, talking to each other or carrying books and papers from one room to another.

The citizens of Pig City walked straight toward Mr. Doyle's room, as if they owned the place.

A teacher crossed their path. She looked at them suspiciously.

"It's not fair we have to stay inside during lunch," Nathan complained. "Just because we didn't finish our work."

"Can we go outside?" Debbie asked the teacher.

"No," she said. "You have to finish your work." She continued on her way.

They walked through the yellow curtain.

Quickly and quietly, they turned every Monkey Town desk upside-down. They had to lift each desk up off the floor, then turn it over and gently set it down, so as not to make a lot of noise.

Laura wrote on the blackboard.

¡SλƎꓘИOꓷ SSIꓘ SλƎꓘИOW

As Aaron and Allison turned over Karen's desk, it opened, and papers and books spilled out onto the floor.

Laura told them to stuff all her junk back in her desk. "We don't want to make a mess," she said. "Mr. Doyle might get mad."

# 28
# Truce

*The class was in an uproar.* " 'Monkeys Kiss Donkeys!' " someone shouted. "That's what it says! 'Monkeys Kiss Donkeys!' "

"Quiet!" Mr. Doyle shouted. "My word. Can't you come back from lunch without all this screaming and yelling? There are other classes going on, where, believe it or not, people are trying to do work. I know that sounds silly to most of you, but — Howard, what seems to be the problem?"

"My desk is upside-down," said Howard.

"Well, I'd say you have two choices, Howard. You can either sit on your head, or turn your desk right side up."

Howard chose the latter. The other members of Monkey Town did the same.

Mr. Doyle erased the board and put the number

14 where the number 13 had been.

"A wise person learns from the mistakes of others," he said. "An average person learns from his own mistakes. And a fool never learns. Here is today's homework assignment."

"But it's Friday!" someone complained.

"I'm glad to see you know your days of the week," said Mr. Doyle. "Maybe you'll learn how to tell time and tie your shoes. This is a kindergarten class, isn't it?"

Nobody said anything.

Mr. Doyle piled on the homework.

"It's not fair that we should all be punished because some people's desks were upside-down," someone complained.

"Only the people with upside-down desks should be punished!" said Tiffany.

Mr. Doyle said that it wasn't punishment. He explained that since they had wasted so much time during the day with childish nonsense, they would have to make up the work at home.

"If you waste any more class time," he said, "then you'll have more homework."

Laura knew it was punishment. They had only wasted about fifteen minutes, and he had assigned over an hour's worth of homework. It was punishment, and everyone knew it, and Mr. Doyle knew they knew it, and he wanted them to know it.

When the bell rang, Gabriel came to Laura's desk and asked if he could talk to her alone.

Laura immediately covered her cap with her hand.

"I'm not going to take your cap," Gabriel said. "I just want to talk to you, president to president."

Allison and Tiffany came to her defense.

"I want to talk to Laura, alone," said Gabriel.

"Did you hear somebody say something, Allison?" asked Laura.

"No, I didn't hear anything; did you hear anything, Tiffany?"

"No, I didn't hear anything," said Tiffany.

"Laura," said Gabriel.

"Something smells," said Laura. She held her nose. "What is it?"

"It smells like old garbage," said Allison.

"Like my brother's dirty socks," said Tiffany.

"Laura," Gabriel said again.

"Oh!" Laura exclaimed. "It's Gabriel!"

Allison and Tiffany laughed.

Gabriel stared at Laura.

"Okay," she agreed. "But no tricks."

"No tricks," he promised.

She kept her hand on her cap.

They walked outside to an open area, where Tiffany and Allison could watch but couldn't hear. "What?" she asked.

"I think we should make some rules," said Gabriel.

"Rules?" questioned Laura. "All's fair in — " She stopped herself just in time. The expression was "All's fair in love and war." "What kind of rules?" she asked.

"Mr. Doyle's getting mad," said Gabriel. "If we're not careful, we'll all get kicked out of school. I think we should work out a truce. We could take turns writing on the board instead of risking our lives sneaking in after each other. You have Monday, I have Tuesday, you have Wednesday. . . ."

"I'm not afraid of Mr. Doyle," said Laura.

"The whole class got in trouble today," said Gabriel. "Not just us. I don't think that's fair."

Laura felt bad about that, too. "How do I know I can trust you?" she asked.

"Trust *me*?" Gabriel asked, pointing to himself. "I'm the one who's taking a chance trusting you!"

"What's that's supposed to mean?" Laura demanded.

Gabriel backed off. "Sorry," he said. "We'll just have to trust each other."

"How do I know it's not another one of your tricks?" she asked.

"I said, you can trust me. Look, just because you always lie, that doesn't mean everybody else does."

"What? I never lie!"

"Oh, yeah, right!"

"You're unbelievable," said Laura. She turned her back on him, swishing her hair behind her.

"Laura, look out!" shouted Allison.

She instinctively covered her hat with her hand and crouched down to her knees.

Howard charged into and fell over her.

The members of Pig City rushed to her.

"I'm okay," she told them, getting up. She looked at Howard still on the ground, then at Gabriel. "Oh, yeah, I can trust you, can't I?"

"What are you, a Girl Scout?" he asked.

"I just missed it, Gabe." said Howard.

Laura led Pig City away. Behind them, Monkey Town sang:

"*Monkey Town, Monkey Town. . . .*"

"Monkeys are mustard!" Aaron turned and shouted.

Laura covered her ears and hummed until they were far enough away. "We need a song!" she declared.

They all agreed.

" 'The Pig City National Anthem,' " said Nathan.

They decided that Kristin should write it, since she was the best writer.

"Do you think you can have it by tomorrow?" Laura asked her.

"I guess so," said Kristin.

"Good. Tomorrow we all meet in the Dog House," said Laura. "And I want everybody to bring mustard," she added. "Lots of it. As much mustard as you can get your hands on."

Nathan looked at his hands. "That will be kind of messy, won't it?"

# 29
# Mustard!

*Laura opened* the refrigerator door.

"Can I make you something?" asked her mother.

Laura pulled out a jar of mustard. "Is this all the mustard we have?" she asked. The large jar was more than half full.

Her mother laughed. "How much do you need?"

"A bunch of kids are coming over," Laura explained.

"Well, I think that should be enough," said her mother. "Now what do you want *with* your mustard? I can put some corn dogs in the microwave."

"Nothing, just mustard," said Laura. She took it to the back door. "I'll be in the Dog House."

"Laura!" said her mother.

"What?"

Her mother stared at her a moment then shook

her head. "Nothing." She shrugged. "When I was a girl I used to eat peanut butter straight from the jar."

"How gross!" said Laura. She opened the back door.

"On your way, if you don't mind, would you move the sprinkler to over by the rosebushes? Thank you."

The lawn sprinkler was in the middle of the yard, spewing water in all directions. Laura set the jar down, then reached behind a shrub and turned off the water. She moved the sprinkler next to the three yellow rosebushes at the side of the yard. She turned the water back on, then took her mustard to the Dog House. There's a lot more you can do with mustard, she thought, besides put it on a corn dog!

Within a half hour everyone arrived — with mustard.

"We had four different kinds," said Aaron. "This one's French mustard; this one has brown sugar and horseradish. . . ."

"Yuck-ola," said Allison.

"This one's got wine and garlic," Aaron continued, "and this one has dill." He passed his unusual mustard around for the others to smell.

"Your mother's crazy," said Debbie. "No offense."

"Now what'd she do?" asked Laura.

"She told me that next time, I didn't have to bring my own mustard. She said she had plenty of mustard here, *all I could eat*. What does she think I'm going to do? Eat this stuff right out of the jar?"

"She told me the same thing," said Nathan.

"She eats peanut butter out of the jar, too," said Laura.

All the mustard was set down on the coffee table, some in jars and some in plastic bags.

"So what's the plan?" asked Debbie.

"We can rub it in their hair," suggested Nathan.

"Stick it in their shoes!" laughed Allison.

"And their desks," said Aaron.

"Down their pants," said Tiffany. She lay flopped across the purple bean bag chair.

Laura sat still in the swinging chair. "We're going to *divide* and *conquer*!" she said.

Nobody looked very impressed. Laura was a little disappointed, but she knew they'd like her plan once they heard all the details.

"Okay. First, we have to learn our song," she said. "Do you have it, Kristin?"

Kristin nodded. She was so nervous, she hadn't said a word since she arrived.

"Well, let's hear it!" said Tiffany.

Kristin stood next to the television. "See, since it's our national anthem, I wanted to make it sound patriotic."

"That's good!" said Nathan.

"So, it's the same tune as 'Yankee Doodle.' " She closed her eyes, took a deep breath, opened her eyes, and sang:

*"Laura Sibbie went to class.*
*Her hair was long and pretty.*
*Stuck a feather in her cap,*
*And called it Pig City!"*

She smiled, then took another breath.

*"Pig City is the best!*
  *Monkey Town is mustard!*
  *They're uglier than Mr. West,*
  *And mushier than custard!"*

She blushed. "That's it."

Everyone clapped their hands.

"That's great, Kristin!" said Nathan.

"It's a lot better than the Monkey Town song!" said Allison.

"It's the best song I ever heard," said Aaron.

Kristin beamed.

Wait till Gabriel hears that! thought Laura.

"Who's Mr. West?" asked Tiffany.

"Who?" asked Aaron.

"She sang they were uglier than Mr. West," said Tiffany. "So, who's Mr. West?"

"Oh," said Kristin.

"Who is he?" asked Debbie.

"I don't know," Kristin admitted. "I couldn't think of anything else to rhyme with 'best.' Do you think it matters?"

"No, there's probably a Mr. West somewhere who's ugly," said Nathan.

"That's what I thought," said Kristin.

"It's a common last name," Tiffany agreed.

They all agreed it didn't matter. They memorized the words, then rehearsed it until they could sing it perfectly. Every time they finished, somebody would shout, "One more time!"

*"Laura Sibbie went to class.*
  *Her hair was long and pretty.*
  *Stuck a —"*

128

The door burst open.

"Now!" Gabriel hollered. He was standing in the doorway without a shirt. In his hands he held the lawn sprinkler, turned off and pointed away from him. The water shot out. "All the way!" he yelled.

The members of Pig City scrambled over each other and onto the bed against the wall. It was safe there. The water didn't quite reach that far and the hose was stretched as far as it would go. Gabriel was the only one who got wet.

In the backyard, Monkey Town sang:

*"Monkey Town! (clap-clap)*
*Monkey Town! (clap-clap)*
*We're the greatest club around! (clap-clap)*
*Chicken Pigs! (clap-clap)*
*Chicken Pigs! (clap-clap)*
*They lay eggs and suck on figs!"*

Gabriel set the sprinkler down just inside the clubhouse door, then jumped back, out of the spray of the water. "Let's go!" he shouted.

The singing stopped.

Pig City were huddled together on the bed. "Somebody get that thing out of here!" shouted Laura.

She was against the wall, behind Kristin, who was behind Aaron. Nathan was on one side of her and Allison on the other. For the most part, everyone was dry. Only an occasional drop of water reached the bed, but the Dog House was being drenched.

Nobody moved.

"Help! Help!" called Allison and Aaron.

"Shut up!" said Laura. "Monkey Town might still be out there. Do you want them to hear you?"

During the stampede to the bed, someone had kicked over the coffee table, and the mustard fell to the floor. Jars broke and plastic bags opened.

Mustard water with horseradish, brown sugar, garlic, wine, dill, and whatever else oozed across the floor.

"Aaron!" Laura shouted. "You're closest!"

"My clothes will be ruined," he said. "I have to walk home. You live here. You can change into dry clothes."

"I can't move!" said Laura. "I'm stuck behind Kristin."

"And I'm stuck behind Aaron!" said Kristin.

Drops splattered the yellow floor.

"Look out, I'm coming through!" said Laura. She pushed into Kristin.

Aaron, Kristin, and Tiffany got tangled together and all three fell into the yellow swamp as Laura jumped off the bed. She ran headfirst into the thick spray. She picked up the sprinkler and hurled it away.

Monkey Town was gone.

She walked to the back door and turned off the water.

The citizens of Pig City dripped out of the Dog House, one at a time.

Laura sadly shook her head. She felt ashamed. The clubhouse had practically been destroyed. She saw Gabriel's shirt lying on the back stoop. She realized he must have taken it off so it wouldn't get wet, then forgot it. She stepped on it.

"Now what are we going to do?" asked Kristin.

"We have no choice," said Laura. "We have to surrender." She took off her wet cap.

# 30
# Terms of Surrender

*There was no school* Monday because it was Memorial Day. On Tuesday when Laura came to school, she didn't write on the blackboard. That wasn't the kind of thing a person who was about to surrender would do. She just walked into class along with everyone else. She held her hat in her hand.

PIGS ARE ALL WET was written on the blackboard. Mr. Doyle erased it, then put the number 15 next to the rectangle. He told the class to pass their homework forward.

Laura opened her notebook and took out several pieces of paper. She gave all but one to the girl in front of her.

She nervously looked over the page she kept. She had worked harder on it than she had on all her homework. She read it for the hundredth time.

*Dear Jonathan,*

*This is a very difficult letter for me to write. It seems that the time has come for Pig City to surrender. It is foolish for us to fight if you're going to win in the end. We might all get kicked out of school if we're not careful. Meet me at the swings at the beginning of recess so we can discuss the terms of surrender. Come alone. As I'm sure you can understand, this must be kept confidential until all the terms are settled.*

> *Bravely,*
> *Laura Sibbie*
> *President of Pig City*

As she said, it had been a very difficult letter for her to write. She had to be careful that nothing she wrote was a lie.

Now, she had to think of a way of getting it to Jonathan. She didn't dare let Mr. Doyle see it.

"Laura, will you come here, please," said Mr. Doyle.

Laura smiled. That was easy, she thought. She put the note in her back pocket and walked to Mr. Doyle's desk.

"You're not wearing your hat," he said to her.

"So?"

"You've worn it every day for a month. I was just wondering — "

"There's no rule saying I have to wear my cap, is there? Nobody else has to to wear a cap to class; why do I?"

Mr. Doyle shrugged. "You don't," he said. "I'd gotten used to it, that's all." He smiled. "I liked it. I apologize."

Laura turned and walked away, swishing her hair behind her. She was glad Mr. Doyle liked her cap. On her way back to her seat, she took the note out of her back pocket and placed it in front of Jonathan, on his desk.

He quickly covered it with his notebook.

At recess, she walked out to the swing set alone. The lower grades had recess at a different time than the upper grades, so the swings were empty.

She sat on the swing in the middle and slowly swung back and forth, dragging her feet in the dirt. Her cap was on her lap.

Jonathan walked out to meet her, tall and proud.

"Thank you for coming alone," said Laura. "This would be a lot more difficult if everyone was here clowning around."

"I understand," Jonathan said very seriously. Ulysses S. Grant didn't laugh at Robert E. Lee at Appomattox.

"May I see the note I gave you?" she asked.

He handed it to her. She looked at it quickly, then put it in her pocket.

"As I said, if we're not careful, we might all get in trouble. Therefore, I think it's important for both clubs that the terms of surrender be fair and reasonable."

Jonathan smiled. He had an evil gleam in his eye. "We won't demand too much from you," he said. "Maybe you'll have to be our slaves for a day."

"That's a possibility," said Laura. "First, I want to make one thing clear. As president of Pig City, I have the power to agree to terms with you, and the rest of Pig City will have to do what I say. Do you have the same power?"

"What do you mean?"

"Well, this works both ways," said Laura. "Will the other members of Monkey Town automatically agree to whatever you say?"

Jonathan thought a moment. "Well, as you know, I didn't tell anybody about this meeting. You said to keep it confidential. So we didn't discuss what power I had."

Laura sighed disgustedly. "Are you the president of Monkey Town or aren't you?" she demanded.

Jonathan looked up and down and from side to side. "Well, yes, sort of. I'm not actually the president of Monkey Town," he admitted. "But that doesn't matter. I — "

"You're not?" questioned Laura. "Who is?"

"Gabriel."

"Gabriel!" Laura exploded. "Gabriel tells *you* what to do? Gabriel orders you around?"

"Well, he doesn't *order* me. . . . I mean, we're all pretty equal."

"*Gabriel!*" she repeated. "I just assumed. . . ." She shook her head. ". . . I'm sorry, but I can only surrender to the president of Monkey Town."

"It doesn't really matter who the president is," said Jonathan.

"It does to me," said Laura. "*Gabriel!* What a joke!" She forced a laugh. "How did he ever get to be president over you? Was there a vote?"

"No. He started the club so — "

"You should demand a vote," she told him. "You know you're better than Gabriel. If they don't make

135

you president, you should start your own club. Lion's Den! That's more like you, anyway. Gabriel's a monkey. You're a lion!"

"Well, maybe. I don't know," said Jonathan.

"I do," said Laura as she hopped off the swing. "I know I'm not going to surrender now, now that you've said Gabriel is president! What a joke!" She walked away, swishing her long hair behind her.

She hadn't lied. She wasn't going to surrender *now*. Of course she wasn't going to surrender *before*, either. Her plan was the same as it had always been: *Divide* and *Conquer!*

She knew that Gabriel was president of Monkey Town. He had told her that when he had tried to trick her into agreeing to a truce. But it isn't a lie to ask a question, even if you already know the answer.

She brushed back her hair and put on her cap.

# 31
# Division

*The citizens of Monkey Town* argued with each other all during lunch. Gabriel, Sheila, Karen, and Howard were on one side. Jonathan, Yolanda, and Howard were on the other.

Howard agreed with everything anybody said.

Jonathan told them that if he was president, Pig City would have surrendered already. "They'd have to do whatever we ordered them to do," he stated. "Laura was begging for mercy until she found out *Gabriel* was president."

"You said she gave you a note," said Karen, peeling an orange. "Let's see it."

"She took the note back."

"Without the note, you have no proof," said Sheila.

"He doesn't need proof," said Yolanda.

"Jonathan wouldn't lie," Howard agreed.

"Why would she want the note back?" asked Sheila. "If she was going to surrender anyway?"

"I'll tell you why," said Gabriel. "She probably said everything Jonathan said she said, but Laura's a stinking liar. She wants us to fight with each other, just like we're doing. She tricked you, Jonathan, just like she once tricked me. She made a fool out of you, too."

"You're the fool, Gabriel, not me," said Jonathan.

"Laura would never surrender," said Karen.

"If Jonathan was president, she would," said Yolanda.

"They'd be our slaves," said Jonathan.

"Then why won't she surrender to Gabriel?" asked Sheila.

"Because Gabriel's a joke," said Jonathan.

"Hey!" said Gabriel.

"That's what Laura said," said Jonathan. "I didn't say it."

"Okay," said Gabriel.

"But it's true," Jonathan added.

"Gabriel started the club," said Karen. "He led the attack on their clubhouse!"

"You've done a great job so far, Gabe," Howard agreed. "That's why Laura wants to surrender, because of what you've done."

"Gabriel's done okay," Jonathan admitted. "I could have done better, but. . . ." He shrugged. "The important thing is Laura won't surrender so long as Gabriel's president."

"She'll never surrender, anyway," said Karen.

"Gabriel's our president," said Sheila.

"We never voted," said Yolanda.

They voted. Gabriel won four to three. Howard voted twice.

Jonathan quit. "I don't take orders from Gabriel!" he asserted. "I'm starting a new club — Eagle's Nest!" He and Yolanda walked away, hand in hand.

Howard ran after them. "Let me join Eagle's Nest, too, Jonathan? Gabriel's a fool!"

"You voted for him, Howard," said Yolanda.

"I voted harder for Jonathan."

"Sorry, Howard," said Jonathan. "You're not good enough to be in Eagle's Nest."

Howard returned to Monkey Town. He stuck his thumb in his ear and wiggled his fingers. "Boy, Jonathan and Yolanda are so conceited," he said. "We're better off without them. I never believed Laura wrote him a note."

"Get lost, traitor," said Karen.

"I didn't want to join Eagle's Nest." Howard tried to explain. "I was going to spy on them for you guys."

Sheila snorted.

" 'Bye, Howard," Gabriel said coldly.

Laura folded her arms in front of her. "What do you want?" she asked.

"Can I join Pig City?" asked Howard.

It was still lunchtime. Everyone, except Aaron, had finished eating.

Howard told them all about Monkey Town's civil war. He said he didn't want to join either Monkey Town or Eagle's Nest. He said he wanted to be a member of Pig City!

They questioned him until he told them everything he knew about the two clubs. He showed them the secret Monkey Town salute.

Laura thought it was the silliest thing she'd ever seen.

"So when can I join Pig City?" he asked.

Laura decided he had no more useful information. "Never," she said.

"Kiss off," said Debbie.

Everyone put their thumbs in their ears and wiggled their fingers at him.

He sadly walked away.

"We should've told him he could join," said Tiffany. "Then we could have taken him to the clubhouse and mustardized him!"

They all laughed.

"Howard's not worth it," said Laura. "I'm saving my mustard for Gabriel."

# 32
# Nice

"*Let's cut off* all her hair," suggested Sheila.

"What?" asked Gabriel. "Are you crazy?"

"You have any better suggestions?" Sheila asked.

Gabriel sadly shook his head. There was nothing to do. He was out of ideas.

"Uh-oh, here they come," said Karen.

"Just ignore them," said Sheila.

They headed home. Pig City followed and sang:

> "*Laura Sibbie went to class,*
> *Her hair was long and pretty.*
> *Stuck a feather in her cap,*
> *And called it Pig City!*
> *Pig City is the best!*
> *Monkey Town is mustard!*

"One more time!" shouted Kristin.

After having to listen to the song three more times, Gabriel, Karen, and Sheila finally were left alone.

"I have a plan so we'd never get caught," said Sheila.

"Who's Mr. West?" asked Karen.

"What? Who?" asked Gabriel.

Karen sang: " 'They're ug-li-er than Mr. West.' " She spoke: "So, who's Mr. West?"

"I don't know," said Gabriel, "and I don't care."

"Don't you two know anything?" asked Sheila. "Mr. West owns the computer store in the mall. He sold us our home computer."

"Is he ugly?" asked Karen.

"Ughh, he's gross," said Sheila.

"Let's go to the mall!" urged Karen. "I want to see him."

"Look, do you want to hear my plan or not?" asked Sheila.

"What plan?" asked Gabriel.

"Okay, Laura has to walk to school alone, so she can get there early to write on the board, right? On her way, she walks past the Hollow Creek apartment complex. There's a short brick wall that separates the apartment complex from the sidewalk. We can hide behind that. Then when Laura walks by, we can reach over the wall and cut off her hair. She won't even feel it. She'll just keep on walking to school while her hair remains in a lump on the sidewalk behind her."

Gabriel and Karen stared at her, eyes wide.

Sheila continued. "She won't know anything is wrong until she sees herself in a mirror! And she'll never know how it happened. She'll wonder about it her whole life, until she's old and gray. 'Her hair was long and pretty,' " she said snidely. "You know Laura wrote that song. She's so vain. I know I wouldn't want hair like hers. I'd have to wash it every day. Laura never washes it. That's why it's so smelly and matted."

"You're bonkers!" said Karen.

"No, wait! I got a better idea!" Sheila exclaimed. "After she walks away, we can pick up her hair and then put it in Jonathan's desk. He'll get blamed for it. We'll get Pig City and Eagle's Nest at the same time! It's perfect."

Gabriel didn't think so.

"What's wrong with it?" Sheila demanded.

"It isn't . . ." said Gabriel. He tried to find the right word. "It's not . . . nice."

"Nice?" asked Sheila. "*Nice?* You're sick!"

"I mean," Gabriel tried to explain. "You know, breaking pencils is one thing, but cutting off her hair? That's cruel. We're all going to graduate in two weeks. Why be mean?"

"I should have voted for Jonathan," said Sheila. " '*It's not nice,*' " she said mockingly. She snorted, then stormed away.

Gabriel and Karen took turns kicking a rock as they continued walking.

"Thanks for voting for me," said Gabriel. "I know you and Yolanda are best friends."

"You started the club," said Karen. "And you were the one who led the attack against Pig City. And," she smiled, "you're nice."

" 'Yankee Doodle' used to be my favorite song," Gabriel said sadly.

# 33
# Conquer!

*Laura and her friends* helped her mother carry nine bags of groceries in from the car. They set them down on the kitchen counter.

"Did you buy any mustard?" Laura asked.

"As a matter of fact I did," said her mother. "I know how much you and your friends all like it, so I bought two big jars. That ought to last you a — "

"Thanks!" said Laura. She found the sack with the mustard and handed one jar to Tiffany and one to Kristin.

"Yeah, thanks, Mrs. Sibbie," said Tiffany.

They all thanked her. Allison took several spoons out of the silverware drawer.

Laura told everybody to wait for her out front, then she went into her room. She got Gabriel's

145

shirt with her footprint on it out from the bottom of her sweater drawer. She got something else, too. It was the note he had put in her desk a long, long, long time ago.

> *Hey Laura,*
> *I know all about Pig City. If you don't kiss me I will tell the whole school. You have ugly hair.*
> > *Your humble servant,*
> > *Gabriel*

She stuck the note in her back pocket, then joined her friends out front.

They went to Gabriel's house.

Laura walked to the front door carrying his shirt. Everyone else hid behind a car parked in the driveway next door. She rang the doorbell.

Gabriel opened the door.

"I came to return your shirt," said Laura.

He stared at her.

She stepped back, off the front stoop.

Gabriel stepped out of the house, onto the stoop.

"First, I want to show you something," said Laura. She took another step back, then took the note out of her back pocket.

"What's that?" he asked.

"The note you wrote me," she said. "I just want to prove to you that I know you're the liar."

Gabriel put his hands on his hips and sighed disgustedly.

"Do you want to see it or not?" she asked. She turned her back on him and stepped out onto the lawn, swishing her hair behind her.

He stepped off the stoop. "I already know what it says."

"Then you admit you lied."

"Let me see it."

She held out her hand. He walked to her and took the note from her. He stepped back to read it, still on the front lawn.

Of course it said exactly what Laura said it said. Gabriel knew it would. It was so obvious that she had changed it. He could even see the eraser marks.

As he was reading the note, Tiffany sneaked out from behind the car and knelt down behind him.

He looked up. "Surprise, surprise," he said sarcastically. "I guess I was lying all along."

"Here's your shirt," said Laura. She started to hand it to him, then shoved him hard, over Tiffany.

He fell on his back, then Pig City pounced on him. Nathan, Aaron, and Debbie held him down while Kristin and Allison spooned the mustard out of their jars and dropped clumps of it onto his face and clothes.

He struggled helplessly to get free. He started to shout, but closed his mouth just in time to avoid a spoonful of mustard. A glob covered his nose.

Laura sat by his head. "Over here," she said. "In his hair. I want to give him a shampoo."

He sneezed, blowing tiny particles of mustard in all directions.

Kristin dumped the rest of her jar out on his head. Laura thoroughly rubbed it into his hair.

Tiffany untied Gabriel's sneakers and pulled them off his feet. Allison dropped spoonful after spoonful into each shoe. "His socks, too," Allison said.

They pulled off his socks and filled those with

mustard, as well. Then they managed to put his socks and shoes back onto his kicking feet. Allison tied the shoes tight. Mustard oozed out through the holes for the laces.

Both jars of mustard were emptied.

"Let's get out of here," said Laura.

They took the jars and spoons and hurried away.

Gabriel lay where he was a moment, then sat up and wiped his face with the shirt that Laura had so thoughtfully returned. He stood and walked into his house. Mustard squished between his toes.

# PART THREE

# Gabriel's Revenge

# 34
# Kaput!

*Laura was feeling* pretty spunky after her victory over Gabriel. On the blackboard she wrote:

PIGS ARE PUNCTILIOUS!

She wasn't sure, exactly, what punctilious meant, but she loved the way it sounded. She said it out loud. "Punc-til-i-ous!" The word exploded out of her mouth.

She cautiously looked around. She almost forgot she wasn't allowed to be there. She shrugged it off. Mr. Doyle will never catch me. I'm punctilious!

She thought it meant something like perfect but even more than perfect, super perfect. She walked punctiliously through the school to the outside, whatever that means.

Pig City was waiting for her, fists at noses. She snappily returned the salute.

"When we see Gabriel," Nathan suggested, "let's all start calling him Hot Dog."

Tiffany laughed.

"He won't come today," said Laura. "He wouldn't dare."

"He'll never come to school again!" said Debbie.

"Monkey Town is *kaput*!" said Kristin.

"*Ka-put!*" Nathan repeated. He liked that word almost as much as Laura liked punctilious.

Her message was still on the board, unchanged, when they all walked into class. Gabriel's desk was empty.

"Mr. Doyle?" Linzy asked. "What does punctilious mean?"

Mr. Doyle thought a moment. "I don't know," he said oddly. "Can anyone tell us what it means?"

Nobody raised a hand. Oh, no you don't, thought Laura. You're not going to catch me that easily.

Mr. Doyle asked Linzy to look it up in the dictionary. She reported back that it meant "extra careful."

"How ironic," said Mr. Doyle. "I don't think the person who's been writing on the board has been very punctilious. In fact, I now know who that person is!"

The class buzzed.

Laura wasn't worried.

"Who?" asked Linzy.

Mr. Doyle shook his head. "Not yet," he said. "Tomorrow I will have proof. Twenty-four hours from now I will put the person's name inside the box! Someone will have to copy sixteen dictionary pages."

Laura still wasn't worried.

At recess, Pig City gathered out on the grass. They all talked about what Mr. Doyle had said.

Laura waved it off. "He doesn't have a clue," she told them.

"Look!" exclaimed Kristin. "There's Gabriel."

Gabriel was walking across the playground toward the school building, whistling.

He walked right by them. "Hello, everybody," he said. "Did I miss anything important in class this morning?"

They stared at him, dumbfounded.

"Well, I have to go check in at the office and let them know I'm here," he said. "See you later." He waved and walked away, whistling again.

The members of Pig City looked at each other.

"What in the world?" said Allison.

"He's crazy," said Tiffany.

"Maybe he has mustard on his brain," said Nathan.

Everyone laughed.

Except Laura. He's up to something, she thought. For the first time all day, she worried.

The rest of the day, Gabriel acted in the same manner. He said hello to the members of Pig City when he saw them and even tried to talk and joke with them.

"I think he just wants to be friends," Aaron said during lunch. "He doesn't have any other friends left."

"Let him be friends with Howard and Sheila," said Debbie.

Howard and Sheila were now hanging out together.

Laura didn't think that was it. Gabriel was up to something. I never should have given him back his note, she thought. She could have kicked herself. He knew what he wrote! I didn't need to give him the evidence. But now that he has it, what's he going to do with it?

After school, Gabriel did it again, whatever it was he was doing. "Hi, Laura, Tiffany, Allison," he said.

They ignored him.

"What'd you think of that history test?" he asked. "That was tough, huh? For me, anyway. I didn't have time to study very much because I had to take a bath. I had to wash my hair." He laughed.

"Do you hear something, Laura?" asked Allison. "I don't hear anything."

"I think I hear a bug," said Laura.

"At least it was only mustard in my hair," said Gabriel. "That's not too hard to get out. Not like spaghetti, huh, Tiffany?"

"I don't hear anything, either," said Tiffany.

"Well, I gotta get going," said Gabriel. "See you guys tomorrow." He walked cheerfully away.

"What an idiot," said Allison.

Laura turned pale. "I have to go home," she said suddenly.

"What's wrong?" asked Tiffany.

Laura didn't answer. She hurried away from her friends and raced home. Gabriel's words rattled inside her head: "Not like spaghetti, huh, Tiffany?"

It was all starting to make sense to her. That was why he was late for school! She ran, walked, ran,

154

walked, ran until she reached her house.

Out of breath, she walked around the side of the house to the backyard. She stopped just outside the Dog House. She was afraid to enter. She closed her eyes, crossed her fingers, then opened her eyes. She stepped inside.

Everything seemed to be in order. They had cleaned it up after Monkey Town's attack. She got down on her hands and knees and looked under the bed. The treasure chest was gone.

# 35
# Let's Make a Deal

*Laura picked up* a french fry and dragged it through a blob of ketchup on the edge of her plate. Besides french fries, her plate contained a hamburger and corn on the cob.

"Sorry we don't have anything you like," said her father. "But don't worry, tomorrow I'll make egg salad, liver, and beets, just for you." He was trying to be funny.

Laura didn't laugh. "I'm not hungry," she muttered. She continued to drag the french fry around her plate, leaving a trail of ketchup behind it. She was trying to think of some way to get the treasures back from Gabriel. It seemed hopeless. She was out of tricks.

She wished there were something she could steal

156

from him. Then she'd have something to trade. I never should have given him back the note, she thought. She could have traded the note for the treasure chest. She could have threatened to show it to the whole school. Everyone would know he wanted to kiss her.

That's it! she thought. Maybe he still wants to kiss me. She knew she was pretty. It was possible Gabriel still wanted to kiss her, even after she mustardized him. She'd seen enough movies to know that men like to kiss pretty women, no matter how rotten they are.

It was worth a try, anyway. "May I be excused?" she asked.

Her parents excused her, but warned her not to come back in thirty minutes looking for something to eat.

"I won't," she said. She went into her room and closed the door.

She brought the phone to her bed and pushed the buttons. As she waited for Gabriel to answer, she lifted her cap, shook back her hair, and put the cap back on.

"Hello?" said a girl's voice.

"Hello, I'd like to speak with Gabriel, please."

"GABRIEL!" screamed the girl.

Laura took several deep breaths to try to steady her nerves.

"Hello?" said Gabriel.

"Hello, Gabriel, this is Laura."

There was a moment of silence, then, "Hi, Laura. I was just doing my math homework. Have you started it yet?"

"No. Not yet."

"It's pretty easy, except for the last two problems. They're tricky."

"Oh. Okay."

"I hear we're going to have a movie tomorrow about the solar system. That should be good, don't you think?"

"I know you have it!" said Laura.

"Have *what*?"

"You know what."

"I don't know what you're talking about, Laura. Unless you tell me, I can't — "

Laura sighed. "The treasure chest," she said. "The Treasures of Pig City."

"The Treasures of Pig City? Gee, I don't know. Describe what they look like."

"I don't have to describe them for you. You know what they are. You stole them!"

"I asked you to describe them to me," said Gabriel.

Laura closed her eyes. She knew she had to do whatever Gabriel said until she got the treasures back. She could picture Gabriel smirking at her as she described all the items in the chest, from Aaron's song to Allison's rear end.

He made her recite her Declaration of Love word for word.

"I, Laura Sibbie, declare that — now and forever, that I'm in love with, um, my teacher, Mr. Doyle. Um, I dream about him all the time, um, and if I was older I'd like to marry him." Her face burned.

"Oh, *those* Treasures of Pig City!" said Gabriel.

"What are you going to do with them?"

"Gee, I don't know. I thought maybe I'd bring them to school for show and tell."

"I'll make you a trade," Laura offered.

Gabriel laughed. "What do you have that I want?"

"Me," she whispered.

He laughed harder.

"Please, Gabriel," she pleaded. "Give them back. I'll do anything you say."

"Anything I say?" he asked.

She collected herself. "Within reason."

"You said, *anything.*"

"Anything within reason."

"How do I know I can believe you?"

"You know I never lie!"

"That's right, I forgot. The note you gave me proved I was the one who lied."

"If you bring the treasure chest here, now, I'll do whatever you say, I promise."

"Gee, I can't," said Gabriel. "I'm not allowed out of the house, and none of my friends can come here. You see, I got in trouble for getting mustard all over everything."

"I'm sorry, Gabriel. Really I am. That was a terrible thing we did to you."

"Eat a raw egg."

"What?"

"Eat a raw egg, and you can have your treasures back."

Laura pulled the phone away from her ear, and covered the mouthpiece with her hand. It could have been a lot worse. She brought the phone back to her mouth and said, "Okay."

"Go do it."

"You mean now?"

"Yep."

"How do you know I'll really eat one?"

"Like you said, I know you never lie."

"Okay, I'll be right back. Hang on."

She set the phone on her bed and walked out of her room and into the kitchen. Her parents were putting the dishes into the dishwasher. She opened the refrigerator door.

"Now, she's hungry," said her father. "I knew it."

"Well, don't eat junk," her mother said to her. "Let me put your hamburger in the microwave."

She ignored them. She got an egg from the inside of the refrigerator door and set it down carefully on the counter. The refrigerator door swung shut.

She opened the cabinet above the counter and took out a small juice glass. She cracked the egg into the glass.

Her parents watched in awe. "Is this some kind of experiment for school?" asked her father.

She stared at the blob at the bottom of the glass. For just a second, she considered telling her first lie. It would be simple. She could just tell him she ate it; he'd never know.

She held her nose with one hand and lifted the glass with the other.

"Laura!" exclaimed her mother.

Well, at least it's better than kissing him, she thought. She poured the egg into her mouth and swallowed it whole. It oozed down her throat.

She stuck out her tongue and said, "Ylah."

She went back to her room and picked up the phone. "Gabriel. Are you there?"

There was no answer.

"Gabriel!" she shouted.

"I'm here," he said quietly.

"I did it. I ate a raw egg."

"Good for you, Laura."

"When do I get the treasures back?"

"Soon." He hung up.

She set down the phone. She hoped she could trust him. She had to.

She went to the bathroom and brushed her teeth for ten minutes.

# 36
# Rule #1

*Never eat a raw egg* before going to bed.

Laura tossed and turned all night. She had all kinds of crazy, frightening nightmares.

She dreamed she had come to school naked. She had been worrying so much about Gabriel and the Treasures of Pig City that she hurried to school without remembering to get dressed. It was all the proof Mr. Doyle needed. As soon as he saw her without her clothes, he knew she was the one who who had been writing on the board.

In another dream, she was chased by a horrible monster who wore big red glasses just like Kristin's. At first she thought the monster was cute, but then realized that the glasses *were* Kristin's. The monster had eaten her!

But the dream that scared her the most was the one where she saw her Declaration of Love printed on the front page of the morning newspaper. That wasn't the scary part. When she read it, it didn't say she was in love with Mr. Doyle. It said she loved Gabriel!

She awoke in horror. It must have been the raw egg, she decided. I'll never eat a raw egg before going to bed again.

She went to school, sneaked into Mr. Doyle's room, and wrote PIGS WEAR SHOES! on the blackboard. She laughed as she imagined pigs walking around wearing shoes and socks. She thought it was her funniest message yet.

"Got you!" said Mr. Doyle. He was sitting at his desk, pointing a camera at her. He snapped her picture. "I warned you I'd have proof today," he said. "Yet you persisted in being punctilious. Now you'll have to copy sixteen, no, seventeen pages out of *this* dictionary." He held up the large hardcover dictionary. It had twice as many words per page as the paperback ones.

"But that's the good dictionary," said Laura.

"We're almost through with it," said Mr. Doyle. "Just don't tear out any of the x, y, or z pages. We haven't studied those yet." He took a drink from his cup of coffee.

Laura tried to think of some way out. Wait a second, she realized. We haven't been studying the dictionary.

"It's the raw egg!" she exclaimed.

"What?" asked Mr. Doyle.

"I ate a raw egg last night," she told him. "This

must be another dream. That's why I didn't see you when I entered the room. I hadn't dreamed you yet!"

"Are you sure about that, Laura?" asked Mr. Doyle.

She nodded. Uh-oh! she worried. She looked down, afraid she was naked again, but glad to see that this time at least she had clothes on. Then she noticed what she was wearing. It was her sister's purple and pink muumuu.

She woke up laughing.

She sat up in bed and looked around her room. Her clock radio said 5:29. I tore up that dress, she remembered.

She got out of bed. It was almost time to get up, anyway, and she was afraid to go back to sleep.

As she washed her hair, the clouds left her head and her real worries returned. Could she trust Gabriel? Would Mr. Doyle have proof?

Her answers were yes and no, and she hoped she had them in the right order.

She brushed her hair a hundred times. She got dressed, putting on her cap last. She skipped breakfast. She was too nervous to sit and eat. She walked to school, brave and confident, or at least pretending to be.

She entered the school building through the side door and made her way to Mr. Doyle's room. There was no reason not to continue writing her messages. She refused to let Mr. Doyle intimidate her.

She stopped before the yellow curtain. If he was in there, waiting for her with a camera, she'd tell him she'd come in to get a book.

She stepped inside. He wasn't there.

She had to get a book, anyway. Otherwise, it would have been a lie if she had said what she was going to say, even though she never said it. She didn't have time to figure out whether that made sense or not.

Book in hand, she went to the blackboard and tried to think of something clever to write. Since it might be her last message, she wanted it to be the best one she'd ever written. She remembered she wrote something hilarious in her dream, but couldn't remember what it was.

It came to her: PIGS WEAR SHOES! She started to write it, then stopped. She made a face. That's not funny, she thought.

It was the raw egg!

She wrote PIG POWER on the board, then hurried out of the room, safe.

# 37
# Boxed

*Gabriel was absent.*

Good, thought Laura. She hoped he was putting the treasures back in the Dog House. He better be!

Mr. Doyle waited for everyone to settle into their seats. Without saying a word he got up from behind his desk and walked to the blackboard. He erased PIG POWER, then moved to the side of the board where DICTIONARY was written. He erased the number 16 and wrote 17 in its place. Then, as everyone watched in hushed silence, he began to write something inside the rectangle.

He wrote the letter L, then stepped away.

All of the members of Pig City and former members of Monkey Town turned and looked at Laura.

She held her head high and tried to look brave.

He can't prove it, she tried to tell herself.

Mr. Doyle finished writing the name inside the rectangle. The name was LINZY.

Laura had to look at it three times before she realized it wasn't her name. She felt dizzy with joy.

The citizens of Pig City all turned and smiled at her, fists at noses. She happily returned the salutes.

The rest of the class was going crazy. Everyone was talking — either about how they never would have thought it was Linzy, or how they knew it all the time, or that there was no possible way she could copy seventeen dictionary pages in just eight days.

"I didn't do it!" Linzy wailed. "It wasn't me!"

"Quiet, or I'll make it eighteen!" said Mr. Doyle.

Linzy wiped her eyes.

"You thought I would think it was Laura, didn't you?" asked Mr. Doyle. "Because of her hat. But I knew Laura wouldn't be foolish enough to write those messages when she's wearing a cap that says 'Pig City.' "

Laura smiled. That was just what she thought Mr. Doyle would think.

"You've got to believe me!" Linzy pleaded.

"I told you I'd have proof, and I have it," Mr. Doyle said sternly. He turned to face the class. "My first clue came two weeks ago, when a teacher reported seeing Linzy in the building before school started."

"But I told you, Mr. Doyle," Linzy pleaded. "I just came in to get a book so I could finish my homework."

"Yes, I know what you *told* me, Linzy," said Mr.

Doyle. "At that time, I couldn't prove anything. But that was when I began to suspect you. Still waters run deep, don't they?"

He turned back to the class. "Yesterday the message on the board was 'Pigs Are Punctilious.' You might remember that Linzy asked me what punctilious meant. She thought she was being so clever. Odd, isn't it, Linzy, that you didn't know what it meant, yet you pronounced it perfectly!" He smiled smugly.

Laura could hardly keep from laughing.

"That was when I was sure it was Linzy," Mr. Doyle continued, "but I still needed proof. I got that this morning from the librarian." He reached into the inside pocket of his sports jacket and pulled out a card like the kind found inside library books. "This is the card from *Charlotte's Web*," he said. "Linzy checked out the book a month ago. It is two weeks overdue."

"I thought I returned that book!" sobbed Linzy. "Besides, that doesn't mean anything."

"As most of you know, the main character of *Charlotte's Web* is a pig," Mr. Doyle said. "In the book, Charlotte the spider writes messages on her web telling the world how great the pig is. Sound familiar?"

Linzy covered her face with her hands. "It wasn't me," she whimpered.

Laura no longer thought it was funny. She felt awful.

"You better stop crying and start writing," Mr. Doyle said coldly. "That is, if you want to graduate."

Linzy dropped her head into her arms, which were folded on her desk.

Laura stood up. "Linzy didn't write on the board," she stated. She took off her cap, shook her hair back off her face, and pulled the cap back on. "I did!"

Mr. Doyle smiled. "Thank you, Laura," he said. "That's the proof I wanted. And thank you, Linzy, for your fine performance."

"It was hard to keep from laughing," said Linzy. She turned around and said, "Sorry, Laura. I didn't know it would be you." Her face was free of tears.

Laura remained standing, too stunned to move.

Mr. Doyle erased Linzy's name and put LAURA inside the box.

# 38
# Betrayed

*For the rest* of the morning, Laura sat like a zombie, staring off into space. She was oblivious to all that went on around her. Mr. Doyle had tricked her! How could I have been so stupid? she asked herself again and again. I should have known he never suspected Linzy — his pet!

Worst of all, it happened in front of everybody. She wondered what the members of Pig City thought of her now. She never felt more ashamed in her life.

Seventeen dictionary pages! It might as well have been a million. Today was Thursday. Next Friday was the last day of school. There was no way she'd be able to copy seventeen dictionary pages in just eight days!

She was the last one out of the room for recess. Numbly, she walked outside. The rest of Pig City was waiting for her, fists at noses. Listlessly, she returned the salute.

"I couldn't believe what you did!" said Nathan.

Laura looked sadly down at the ground.

"It was so . . . noble," finished Nathan.

Laura looked up, surprised.

"I was feeling sorry for Linzy," said Debbie, "but I never would have the courage to do what you did. It made me proud to be a member of Pig City."

"The way you stood up like that," said Tiffany: " 'Linzy didn't write on the board, I did!' It gave me goose bumps."

"It was the bravest thing I've ever seen," said Allison.

Laura couldn't believe it. "I was stupid," she said. "Mr. Doyle tricked me."

"You had no way of knowing that," said Kristin. "You sacrificed yourself so an innocent person wouldn't suffer."

"It was noble," said Nathan. "You deserve the Nobel prize!"

"It was like something Martin Luther King or George Washington would have done," said Allison.

Laura felt her eyes swell with tears. She had never told Allison she wanted to be like George Washington.

"I think that was the worst thing a teacher could do," said Debbie. "Mr. Doyle knew how good you are. He used your *goodness* and your *nobleness* to trap you!"

"Hey, that's right!" said Aaron. "He shouldn't be allowed to do that! It's not fair. It's like he's punishing you for being so good."

The more they talked, the more they hated Mr. Doyle, and the more they admired Laura.

"Let me copy your dictionary pages for you," said Tiffany.

"I'll help, too," said Kristin.

"We all will!" said Aaron.

Everyone cheered. Nathan said, "Okee-dokee-do!"

"What Laura wrote on the board, she wrote for all of us!" said Kristin. "She did it for Pig City. And now Pig City won't let her down!"

They all cheered again.

Laura laughed and cried at the same time.

They tried to figure out the best way to divide seventeen by seven.

"Laura shouldn't have to do any," said Debbie. "We'll each do three, and we'll still have one left over!"

"Laura can write on the board again tomorrow!" declared Kristin.

They all laughed.

Laura was proud to have such wonderful friends. She tried to tell them she'd copy her share, too, but she was too choked up to speak.

"Let's copy only pages with dirty words!" Tiffany suggested.

"Are there dirty words in the dictionary?" asked Allison. She was shocked.

"Haven't you ever read the sex page?" asked Tiffany. "It's full of words starting with s-e-x."

"And the definitions are great," Kristin added.

"I'll copy that page," said Tiffany.

"I'll copy the page with 'urine' on it," said Debbie.

They all tried to think of good pages to copy.

"I get 'excrement,' " said Kristin. "And 'dung.'

And 'feces,' too. I'll do those three."

" 'Ass,' " said Nathan. "I know 'ass' is in the dictionary, even if they're just talking about the donkey!"

" 'Tinkle,' " said Debbie.

" 'Buttocks,' " said Aaron.

"Oh, I just thought of a great word," said Allison, "but I can't say it." She blushed.

"Is it a part of the body?" asked Tiffany.

"We should think of a way to get even with Linzy," said Debbie. "She was in on it, too."

"But she said she didn't know it was Laura," said Aaron.

"So? Ignorance is no excuse," said Nathan.

"We'll figure out a way to get Linzy into trouble, this time for real," said Debbie. "No one should make it through the year without copying at least one page."

"Hey!" said Kristin. "What's going on over there?"

There was a big commotion in the center of the playground.

It was Gabriel. He was marching around the blacktop. Music blared out of a huge portable stereo that he held in the air. There was some kind of white cloth hanging from the top of it, like a flag.

As he got closer, the music became clearer.

". . . *pick my nose, pick my nose,*
*I just love to pick my nose,*
*It is so much fun.*"

Aaron turned pale.

"My underpants!" screamed Kristin.

Kristin's underpants were hanging from Ga-

173

briel's stick. That was his flag.

> *"I'm in love with every girl,*
> *Every girl, every girl,*
> *I'm in love with every girl,*
> *In Mr. Doyle's class."*

Aaron covered his ears with his hands and ran.

Kristin rushed toward Gabriel. Tiffany, Allison, Debbie, and Nathan hurried after her.

Laura took a couple of steps, then remained where she was.

Gabriel swung the stick around over his head until Kristin's underpants flew off into the air. A group of boys jumped for them. Kristin screamed. Her underpants were passed from one boy to another as she helplessly chased after them.

At first, the other members of Pig City tried to help her, but they soon had problems of their own as Gabriel continued to pass around the treasures.

"Extra! Extra! Read all about it!" he shouted, holding Tiffany's newspaper high in the air. "Tiffany's Ticklish!"

Tiffany was chased out of the crowd by a mob of would-be ticklers. "It's your fault, Laura!" she shouted as she ran past her.

Laura knew Tiffany was right.

The music started again.

> *"I am such a stupid jerk,*
> *Stupid jerk, stupid jerk. . . ."*

A boy tossed Kristin's underpants up at the basketball hoop. He missed. Several other boys jumped

174

for the rebound. There were several more attempts at the basket, until the underpants finally got stuck — draped over the rim.

*"I don't have a brain."*

Kristin stared forlornly up at her underpants. Her face was streaked with tears. "I hate you, Laura!" she yelled, in a voice Laura hardly recognized.

The ticklers caught up with Tiffany. She rolled around on the grass, laughing herself to pieces.

*"I'm in love with every girl,*
*In Mr. Doyle's class."*

Gabriel took out the tape and put in a new one. "Hey, everybody! Listen to this!"
Everyone quieted down.

*"Hello. May I talk to Howard, please?*
*(I think that was his mother.)"*
*[Laughter]*
*"Howard? Oh, Howard, is it really you? This is . . . your secret admirer. I love you, Howard. You're so handsome."*
*("Passionately.")*
*"I love you passionately!*
*"I can't tell you. I'm afraid you'll break my heart."*
*[Laughter]*
*"That was Debbie. She just called Howard and told him she loved him passionately, didn't you, Debbie?"*
*"Yes. That was me. I'm Debbie. I disguised my voice because I love Howard so much, and*

I'm afraid he won't love me back.''
[*Laughter*]

The crowd was hysterical. Everyone jeered at Debbie as she ran to the girls' bathroom.

The yard teacher put her hand on Gabriel's shoulder. She took the boom box from him, then collected the other treasures, except for Kristin's underpants, which she couldn't reach. She made Gabriel sit on a bench for the rest of the recess.

"I trusted you, Laura," said Allison with tears in her eyes.

Laura didn't know what to say.

"The whole school has seen me naked!" Allison sobbed.

"Hey, Allison!" a boy called. "When are you going to be in *Playboy*?"

She covered her face with her hands and ran.

"Uh-oh," said another boy. "It's Laura. We better be good. She might tell her boyfriend—Mr. Doyle."

They laughed.

"Will you invite us to the wedding?"

"How many children are you going to have?"

When the bell rang, she headed back to class alone. She wasn't George Washington or Martin Luther King anymore. She was Richard Nixon.

"Well, don't expect me to copy any of your dictionary pages for you," Aaron said to her.

"I don't," said Laura. "I don't expect anything from anybody."

"Hi, Laura, what's new?" asked Gabriel. He was stretched out on the bench with his hands behind his head, smiling smugly.

# 39
# Judgment Day

*Gabriel wrote his name* on the blackboard under the word DICTIONARY, just beneath the box with LAURA in it. He walked proudly back to his seat.

Everyone else remained absolutely silent as Mr. Doyle looked through the Treasures of Pig City laid out across his desk. No one dared laugh.

"Kristin," said Mr. Doyle.

"Yes, sir."

"Your underpants are in the office. You can pick them up after school."

"Yes, sir."

"In the future," he said, "keep them *under* your pants. That's why they're called *under*pants. A word to the wise."

Still, no one laughed.

"Allison, will you come here, please."

Allison's face was red with embarrassment as she stood up in front of a room full of kids, all of whom had seen her naked. She walked to Mr. Doyle's desk.

"You were a very cute baby," he said. He returned her picture to her.

"Thank you," said Allison. She tore the picture to bits and dropped it in the trash, then returned to her seat.

"Nathan!" Mr. Doyle thundered.

Nathan shut his eyes tight, scrunching his face. Up to now, he was the only one who had been spared. He stood and slowly walked to meet his doom.

"Did you write this?" asked Mr. Doyle.

He scrunched his face even tighter as he looked at his letter.

*Dear Mr. Doyle,*
   *You stink. You are the most ugliest teacher in the school! Your too stupid to be a teacher! And you have bad breath. I hate you.*
          *Sincerely,*
          *Nathan*

"Yes, sir," he squeaked.

Mr. Doyle frowned and shook his head. "Do you realize how bad this is?" he asked.

"It wasn't wise, was it?" said Nathan.

"No, it wasn't," said Mr. Doyle. "'Most ugliest'? You know better than that, Nathan. It's either 'ugliest' or 'most ugly,' but never 'most ugliest.' We studied superlatives at the beginning of the year."

Nathan's face slowly unscrunched.

"Look how you spelled 'your,' " Mr. Doyle continued. " 'Your too stupid to be a teacher!'

"When you spell 'your' that way, it's a possessive: your book, your house, your foot. In this letter, you meant to use it as a contraction for 'you are,' didn't you?"

"Um, I guess so."

"Then, how would it have been applied?"

"Um." Nathan wiped his face. "Y-o-u-apostrophe-r-e."

"Why didn't you spell it correctly the first time?"

Nathan shrugged.

"I don't know what's the matter with you, Nathan. You're about to graduate, and you've forgotten everything you've learned. Look at this.

" 'Your too stupid to be a teacher! And you have bad breath.'

"Never begin a sentence with the word 'and.' You could have made it all one sentence: 'You're too stupid to be a teacher, and you have bad breath,' or else you could have kept it as two sentences but without the word 'and': 'You're too stupid to be a teacher. You have bad breath.' Do you see what I'm saying?"

Nathan nodded.

"Okay, now I want you to go to your seat and rewrite this letter so that there are no mistakes."

Nathan returned to his desk. His eyes appeared to be spinning.

"Aaron."

"Yes, Mr. Doyle." His face was red.

"I was able to hear this tape during recess. Do you want it erased, or shall I have it for posterity?"

"Erase it." It became redder.

"Are you certain? You have a very nice voice. Have you ever taken singing lessons?"

"No. Erase it, please." And redder.

"Do you like the opera?"

"I never heard it." And redder.

"You should listen to it some time," said Mr. Doyle. "You might consider being an opera singer when you grow up."

"I'll think about it," said Aaron. "Please erase the tape."

Mr. Doyle put the tape back into the machine and erased it. "Debbie?"

"Erase it," said Debbie.

"Can I have it?" chirped Howard.

Mr. Doyle erased Debbie's tape. "Tiffany."

Tiffany walked to his desk. He told her it was a very funny article. She didn't agree. She threw it into the trash.

"Laura!" Mr. Doyle bellowed.

Laura shook her hair back. She wasn't wearing the cap. It was stuffed in her desk. She walked to the front of the room.

She saw her Declaration of Love on Mr. Doyle's desk. She wasn't embarrassed. She felt nothing — except hatred for Gabriel.

The Pig City roster was on his desk, too.

PIG CITY

*Laura — President*
*Tiffany — Vice-President*
*Allison — Secretary*
*Kristin — underpants*

*Debbie — called up Howard and told him she loved him passionately*
*Yolanda — note to Jonathan*
*Nathan — letter to Mr. Doyle*
*Aaron — song*

"What happened to Yolanda's note?" asked Mr. Doyle.

"What do you need that for?"

"I was just curious." He smiled. "I imagine it was quite a note. You're right, it's none of my business. Well, you've had a rough time of it today, haven't you? First the dictionary pages and now this. I suppose everybody in Pig City blames you."

"I'm responsible," she said.

"I guess that's what being a leader is all about, isn't it?" He picked up the Declaration of Love. "I'm very flattered."

She shrugged.

"Seventeen dictionary pages is a lot, isn't it?" he said. "I can't very well ask someone who loves me to copy that many." He smiled. "How about if we just call it seven?"

"No, I'll do seventeen," said Laura. "I don't love you anymore." She dropped her Declaration into the wastebasket and returned to her seat.

# 40
# Bushwhacked

*Gabriel was the most popular* kid at school. Even Jonathan and Yolanda were impressed by what he had done.

"You were fantastic, Gabe!" said Howard. "Can I please have your autograph?" He handed Gabriel a torn sheet of notebook paper and a pencil.

Gabriel smiled. He took the paper and pencil from Howard and boldly signed his name. "Here you go, Howard."

"Thanks, Gabe!" said Howard. "I bet you'll be famous some day."

Gabriel laughed.

"Howard, do you want to copy a dictionary page, too?" asked Mr. Doyle.

"No," said Howard. He hurried out of the room.

Mr. Doyle followed him out, leaving only Gabriel and Laura.

No one from Pig City had spoken to Laura since recess. They'd been teased and/or tickled all day. Anybody who didn't know about the treasures soon found out.

Laura stood up and walked to the metal closet. She tore seventeen pages out of a dictionary, one at a time. She didn't bother looking for pages with pictures or bad words. She returned to her desk without even glancing at Gabriel.

Sheila was waiting for Howard by the bike racks. "Did you get it?" she asked.

"No problem," he said, then gave her the piece of paper with Gabriel's autograph on it.

Sheila looked at it. "Good job."

"Thanks," said Howard. "Hey, Sheila?"

"What?"

"Do you think Debbie really likes me?"

"Of course not! Why would she like *you*?"

Laura looked up as Gabriel put his completed dictionary pages on Mr. Doyle's desk. She tried to burn a hole through his brain with her eyes.

He turned and faced her. "What's your problem?" he asked.

She didn't say anything.

He shrugged, took a couple of steps toward the curtain, then stopped. He sighed and turned around. "If you want, I'll help you copy some of your dictionary pages. I mean, I wrote on the board, too."

"Go away," she said coldly. "I hate you!"

"Don't tell me you thought I believed you ate a raw egg."

"I never lie."

"Right," said Gabriel. "Just like the note you said I wrote."

"I showed it to you! It proved I was telling the truth."

"Come on. Do you really think I don't know what I wrote? Besides, anyone could see it had been changed."

"I ate the egg."

"Tell me another one!" He walked out through the curtain.

She hated him. She waited a few minutes to make sure he was gone, then took her seventeen pages and left. She hadn't copied a single word.

I won't do them, she thought as she headed home. Then Mr. Doyle will have to flunk me. Maybe I'll spend my whole life stuck in the sixth grade. She smiled bitterly. That'll show Mr. Doyle! He'll be sorry he ever did this to me. She imagined herself twenty years old, in Mr. Doyle's class, still owing him seventeen dictionary pages. "I'm sorry I ever tricked you," he'd say. "Let me copy your dictionary pages for you." "No," she'd tell him. "I can't graduate until I copy them myself. It's your fault. You made the rules."

She'd be in all the newspapers: TWENTY-YEAR-OLD GIRL STUCK IN SIXTH GRADE! Everybody would know about the mean trick Mr. Doyle played on her, how he used her goodness and turned it around to suit his own evil purposes. He'd be the most hated man in the country.

She sighed. She didn't really hate Mr. Doyle. She

didn't love him, but she didn't hate him, either. She hated Gabriel.

"I hate Gabriel!" she shouted to an empty street.

She wondered if she'd ever meet a boy she'd like. The boys will be more mature next year in junior high, she thought. I'll have lots of boyfriends — if I ever graduate.

She walked past the Hollow Creek apartment complex. There was a brick wall, about four feet high, which separated the apartment complex from the sidewalk.

She wondered what her first boyfriend would look like. He'll have dark hair, maybe a little curly. He'll be smart, but he wouldn't study all the time. He'd be good at sports, and he'd also be interested in other things, like art and books. And he'll beat up Gabriel.

She smiled, then suddenly her head jerked back and banged against the brick wall. "Oh!" she said very quietly.

Someone was pulling her hair from behind the wall. She couldn't turn around. She tried to reach back with her arms. Her eyes watered from the pain.

Suddenly the pulling stopped and she fell to her knees on the sidewalk. She felt dizzy. She sat up against the wall, and took several deep breaths. Her head throbbed.

A great mass of hair lay on the sidewalk next to her.

She didn't know what it was at first. It was very odd-looking, like some kind of strange animal. It took her a while to recognize it as hair. A few seconds later she realized where it came from.

# 41
# A Wig

*Laura felt the top* of her head, then slowly moved her hand down along her hair until she came to the place where it had been cut — just above her shoulders.

It had been cut with scissors, although at the time it had felt like someone just ripped it out of her head.

Not all her hair was cut off. Long strands still remained on either side of her head. But a large clump out of the middle was gone.

On the sidewalk, next to her hair, she saw a torn piece of notebook paper. She picked it up.

On it was written: PIGS ARE BALD.

Underneath that, Gabriel had signed his name.

Laura's blood curdled with hatred. She trembled, then tears began to flow. She began gathering up as much of her hair off the ground as she could. In the end, she could barely see through her watery eyes as she picked up the hairs, one at a time, off the dirty sidewalk. Maybe somebody can make a wig out of it, she hoped. I can wear it until my hair grows back.

She stood up, then a wave of dizziness rushed over her. She steadied herself, then started home, walking, then running, then walking again.

She came to a block where garbage cans had been set on the curb in front of each house. The cans were empty. The garbage men had come and gone.

She made it halfway down the block, then stopped. She dropped her hair into an old silver trash can. She leaned over and looked at it, swirled at the bottom, for the last time.

When she got home, she took two steps inside the house, then ran into her mother's arms.

Her mother telephoned her father, who rushed home from work early.

"Do you know who did it?" asked her father.

"No," she answered. It was her first lie in six years, but so what? Her hair was cut off anyway. She could lie all the time now!

Her parents took her to the doctor to make sure she wasn't seriously hurt.

The doctor said she was fine. She had a bump on the back of her head, but no concussion.

"Do I have to go to school tomorrow?" Laura asked.

"Yes," the doctor told her.

"No," her parents said sympathetically.

The doctor suggested that they report the assault

to the police, but Laura talked her parents out of it.

What are they going to do? she thought. Arrest Gabriel for giving me an illegal haircut?

She remembered that Gabriel had tried to call a truce. She was the one who had told him there were no rules in a war.

She went to bed early. It had been the worst day of her life, and she didn't want it to drag on any longer. In the morning, she'd have to get started on her dictionary pages.

Her parents came in and kissed her good-night as she lay with head on her pillow.

"Tomorrow we'll go to the beauty parlor," said her mother.

"They'll just cut off more!" she whined.

"Oh, just enough to make it even," said her father.

"We'll go to the fanciest, most expensive hair-stylist in town," said her mother. "It'll be very exciting. We'll get you something very exotic."

Laura tried to smile. "At least I won't have to spend an hour washing and combing it every day."

"That's right!" said her father.

"Probably just towel it dry," said her mother.

Laura rolled over, then started crying. "I never told a lie," she whimpered.

"We know, baby," whispered her mother.

# 42
# The Conquering Hero

*Gabriel walked to school* on Friday morning, whistling the Monkey Town song and snapping his fingers.

He was met by Sheila and Howard. They stuck their right thumbs in their right ears and wiggled their fingers. He did the same.

"We got her, Gabe!" said Howard. "We got her even better than you did!"

"What?" he asked. "Who?"

Howard looked at Sheila, then back at Gabriel. "Laura," he said. "You'll see when she comes to school."

"*If* she comes to school," said Sheila. "She's so vain, she probably won't."

"I bet she doesn't come to school for the rest of the year," laughed Howard.

Sheila laughed, too.

"Wha'd you do to her?" asked Gabriel.

Howard looked to Sheila.

"Maybe we shouldn't tell him," said Sheila. "Maybe's he's still in love with her!"

"What?" Gabriel exclaimed. "Me? In love with Laura?"

"I saw the note you wrote her," said Sheila.

"What note?"

"Oh? Was there more than one?" She turned to Howard. "He wrote Laura a note telling her he knew all about Pig City, but promised never, ever, to tell." She put both hands over her heart. "It was so *sweet*!"

Howard laughed.

Things began to click inside Gabriel's head. "*You* changed it," he uttered.

"Didn't she want to kiss you?" laughed Sheila. She told Howard how she had reworded Gabriel's note.

Howard laughed, too. "Who would want to kiss Laura?" he asked. "She's so ugly. She asked me to join Pig City, but I told her to drop dead."

Gabriel laughed. "That's pretty funny, Howie," he said. "So how'd you get her yesterday?"

"We bushwhacked her!" said Howard.

"We cut her hair off!" said Sheila. "Just like I said I would. You and Karen didn't have the guts to do it, but Howard did."

"I held her hair while Sheila cut it off," said Howard.

"She never even saw who did it," said Sheila.

"She's practically bald," laughed Howard.

He was still laughing when Gabriel's fist smashed

into his teeth. He fell to the ground. His lip was bleeding.

Gabriel grabbed Sheila by her shirt collar.

She screamed.

"Hey!" shouted the yard teacher. She started toward them.

"Now you'll be sorry," said Gabriel.

Sheila laughed in his face. "What are you going to do? Tell on me? Are you a tattletale?"

He didn't know what to do. He never told on anyone before.

"You better let me go!" warned Sheila. "Besides, Laura thinks you did it, so you're in on it, too."

"How. . . . Why does she think I did it?"

"Remember that autograph you signed for Howard? I wrote 'Pigs Are Bald' over it and dropped it next to her hair! She'll never love you now!"

"Gabriel!" shouted the yard teacher, hurrying toward them. "Let her go!"

He let go of her. Then he slugged her in the face.

# 43
# The New Laura

*Laura stared at herself* in the bathroom mirror. "I look like a French poodle," she said.

"I don't know of any poodles who spend over a hundred dollars for a haircut," said her father, standing behind her.

She made a face. She didn't recognize herself. "You wasted your money," she said. "You should have just taken me to the Pink Poodle. That's where Allison's dog gets his hair cut."

Her father laughed. "*Now* you tell me," he said.

In front, covering her forehead, she had long curly bangs. They looked like springs that had sprung. The rest of her hair formed a big wave that started just behind her bangs and cascaded down to the back of her neck, where it suddenly turned wild and frizzy, like a wave crashing on the shore.

In front of each ear she had a long coil of hair.

Several other coils adorned her hair in various places. They looked like ribbons on a birthday present.

The most amazing thing about it was that all she had to do was wash it, then dry it with a towel, and it would bounce back into shape all by itself.

She stuck out her tongue at her reflection, then turned and walked back into her room.

She sat at her desk. She still hadn't copied any of her dictionary pages. It was Saturday, two days since the worst day of her life. Monday, she'd have to go to school again, where everyone would laugh at her.

She opened her desk drawer, took out her pocket calculator, and busily pressed the buttons. She figured out it would take six years and five months for her hair to grow back. Somewhere she had heard that hair grows three quarters of an inch every month.

She wondered if she'd have any friends by then. She knew she certainly wouldn't have a boyfriend. No boy would want to kiss a French poodle.

Six years and five months, she thought. I might as well be in prison.

She looked through the dictionary pages. Why didn't I at least choose pages with pictures! She shook her head.

She remembered it was Gabriel who had told her about picking pages with pictures. Of course I didn't listen to him! I don't listen to anybody. I think I'm better than everybody else. No one can tell me anything!

I thought Jonathan was conceited, but I was even more conceited than him.

She sighed. It was all my own fault, she realized.

It's no wonder everybody hates me. That's what I get for trying to be such a big shot. Playing all those silly games. Who did I think I was? George Washington? George Washington wouldn't have made someone give him her underpants!

She promised herself that in the future she'd be different. She wouldn't be the president of any club, because she wasn't better than anybody else. No more tricks. No more games. No more lies.

She nodded. I lied all the time, she admitted. Even if my words weren't actual lies, they were lies all the same. I lied to myself, too. I'm glad my hair was cut off. I deserved it! Thank you, Gabriel!

From now on, there will be a new Laura Sibbie, she decided. And maybe, in six years and five months, somebody will like me.

The doorbell rang.

Oh, please, don't be for me, she prayed.

"Laura! There's somebody here to see you," her father called.

She didn't want to see anyone. She didn't want anyone to see her, not for six years and five months.

"Laura!" her father shouted.

She stayed still.

There was a knock on her door, then her father stepped inside. "Laura, you have a visitor," he said.

She gave him a look that said, Can't you tell her I'm not home?

He ignored it.

She shrugged her shoulders, got up from her desk, sighed, then walked out of her bedroom and down the hall.

Gabriel was waiting just inside the front door, holding a bunch of flowers.

# 44
# Kiss Me

*Gabriel stared at her* with his mouth open. "Wow," he uttered. "You look like a movie star."

She waited for him to say something like, "You could play Frankenstein without a mask," but he didn't. He just stared at her hair.

"Um, these are for you," he said. He blushed as he held out the flowers. They were daisies, white with yellow centers.

She took the flowers. She would have ripped them to bits and thrown them in his face, but — nobody had ever given her flowers before. She brought them to her nose.

"They're not the kind that smell," he said.

She stared at him. She wondered how he could dare show his face at her house after what he did to her.

"You could be on the cover of a magazine," said Gabriel. "You look so . . . elegant."

She shook back her hair, although it didn't shake back anymore. She wondered if Gabriel really liked it, or if he was just saying it because he didn't want her to get him in trouble for cutting it.

"From what they said, I thought they practically shaved your head," he said.

"What are you talking about? Who?"

"Howard and Sheila. They're the ones who did it to you. It wasn't me. They tried to frame me by dropping a piece of paper with my name on it."

"It was your handwriting," said Laura.

"I know," said Gabriel. "Howard tricked me into signing it. Can you believe it? *Howard?*" He smiled. "He said he wanted my autograph. I guess that's what I get for thinking I was such a hot shot."

Laura didn't know whether to believe him or not.

"Howard confessed everything to Mr. Doyle," said Gabriel. "I was there. No one else knows anything about it. Boy, you should have seen Mr. Doyle. I thought he was going to kill them. He was so mad at *them*, he didn't punish me for giving Sheila a bloody nose!" He smiled. "Mr. Doyle's all right. I can see why you're in love with him."

"I'm not in love with him," said Laura. "I like him, but I don't love him."

"Oh."

"You gave Sheila a bloody nose?"

"I gave Howard a fat lip, too. I couldn't believe what they did to you. It made me so mad. It was such a mean thing to do, especially since . . ." he paused, ". . . you never told a lie."

196

Laura raised her eyebrows.

"I'm sorry for not believing you."

"But how — "

"Sheila was the one who changed the note. She saw me put it in your desk, and she took it out and changed it. She's the one who wrote that you had to kiss me, or else I'd tell everyone about Pig City. How could, I mean, can't you see why I — "

"You shouldn't have called me a liar."

"I know. I'm sorry."

Laura looked at the flowers, then at Gabriel. "I have a vase in the Dog House."

They walked through the kitchen, out the back door, and across the yard to the clubhouse.

On top of the bookcase was a clear blue vase with a peacock feather in it. Laura removed the feather, dropped it on the floor, and put the daisies in the vase. She placed it back on the bookcase. She figured she'd add water later.

Gabriel sat in the swinging chair.

Laura remembered that that was where he sat the last time he was in the Dog House. She sat on the bed again. "What did the note say before Sheila changed it?"

Gabriel looked down at the ground. "I told you that I knew all about Pig City, but I promised not to tell anybody. I also wrote that you had pretty hair, but then I erased it because. . . ." He blushed. "But I never said it was ugly. Sheila wrote that, too."

"But how did you ever find out about Pig City?"

"Oh," he said. He smiled sheepishly. "I didn't. I heard you and Tiffany and Allison talking about it, but I had no idea what it was. I was hoping the note would trick you into telling me. I'm sorry. I'm always playing tricks on people and then they backfire on me!"

"I know what you mean," Laura grumbled.

"I'm really sorry," he said. "I'm sorry for trying to trick you and for not believing you and for bringing all those treasures to school."

Laura looked at his sad brown eyes.

She wondered what would have happened if Sheila hadn't changed the note. Gabriel's trick probably would have worked. She probably would have asked him to join Pig City. But that wouldn't have been so bad. She wondered what she would have asked him to do for insurance: Wear a dress or kiss her?

But that was the old Laura. The new Laura didn't play those kinds of games.

"When you asked me to join Pig City," he said, "that was the happiest moment of my life. I just wanted you to like me. That's all I ever wanted."

She felt a warm tingle inside her.

"I don't blame you for hating me. If I were you, I'd hate me, too. Even if I weren't you, I'd probably still hate me. I hate myself and I'm me."

She didn't hate him. She knew he didn't do anything she wouldn't have done, if she were him.

"No more tricks!" Gabriel promised. He crossed his heart.

"No more tricks," Laura agreed.

Gabriel shook his head. "I just wish. . . . Is there anything I can do to make it up to you?" he asked.

She held back a smile.

"You don't even have to forgive me. I just don't want you to hate me for the rest of your life."

She thought he had beautiful eyes.

"I'll do anything you say," he said.

She picked up the peacock feather and gently brushed it across the floor. "There is one thing you could do," she said very quietly.

"What?" he asked.

She smiled sweetly. "Eat a raw egg."

# 45
# The Final Bell

*Now they were even.*

The final week of school is usually the most exciting week of the year, but compared to the last four weeks, it was nothing.

Sheila and Howard weren't there. They were suspended from school for the last week, but would still go on to junior high next year.

Everyone had something to say about Laura's new hairstyle. Almost everybody said they liked it, but she didn't care. George Washington didn't care what people said about his hair. Which was a good thing, she thought, since his hair was white and stiff.

On the final day of school, Laura handed in her seventeen completed dictionary pages.

Mr. Doyle was shocked. After all that had happened, he no longer expected her to do them. He thought she knew that.

She did. She did them, anyway. Allison, Tiffany, Gabriel, Kristin, Debbie, Nathan, Aaron, Yolanda, Jonathan, Karen, and even Linzy all helped. Linzy said she felt bad about tricking Laura. Besides, she wanted to find out what it was like to copy a dictionary page.

They'd had a dictionary-page copying party. But if Mr. Doyle ever noticed some of the words they had copied, he'd — well, they didn't know what he'd do. Besides, It would be too late.

Laura's friends liked her again. They even liked Gabriel, since she and he were *together*.

The final bell rang.

Laura was no longer a sixth-grader.

She felt strangely sad as she walked through the yellow curtain for what she thought would be the last time.

"Laura!" Mr. Doyle called after her.

She turned around and stepped back into the room.

Mr. Doyle was standing at attention. His fist was at his nose.

She returned the salute.

# About the Author

Louis Sachar is the author of several children's books, including *Sideways Stories from Wayside School*, *Sideways Arithmetic from Wayside School*, and the Newbery Medal-winning *Holes*.

Louis Sachar is not a member of a secret club—or, at least, he says he isn't. He probably has never eaten a raw egg. He grew up in Tustin, California, where his sixth-grade teacher used to punish kids by making them copy dictionary pages.